REAPER'S RETURN

Book One of the Chronicles of Aesirium

by

Ren Cummins

Dedications:

For Elizabeth and Jillian, who never fail to remind me to dream bigger than the world says is possible;

To Jen, Quiana, Xio, Garth, and Heather, without whose help, friendship and good old fashioned elbow grease, this thing might never have gotten off the ground.

And to this world for being the best place I can imagine to imagine in.

Other books in the Chronicles of Aesirium:
Book Two: The Morrow Stone
Book Three: The City of the Dead
Book Four: Reaper's Flight
Book Five: Through the Blink
Book Six: The Crook and the Blade
Tales of Aesirium

Also:
Into the Dust (with Kiri Callaghan)

The Talaria Press Founders Anthologies:
Quests and Answers
Once More Upon a Time

Contents

Prologue   **7**

Chapter 1: Rom   **9**

Chapter 2: Boots and Bullies   **19**

Chapter 3: Beneath the Watchful Sun   **27**

Chapter 4: The Most Important Thing   **39**

Chapter 5: In the Shadow   **61**

Chapter 6: Cousins   **77**

Chapter 7: The Deal   **91**

Chapter 8: The World of Spirits   **107**

Chapter 9: Only Mostly Dead   **123**

Chapter 10: Remembering Life   **139**

Chapter 11: The Apothecary   **157**

Chapter 12: The Looking Glasses   **171**

Chapter 13: Of Death, Life & In Between   **183**

Chapter 14: Training Begins   **197**

Chapter 15: Drawing the Crook   **209**

Chapter 16: Never Use a Strange Pistol   **221**

Chapter 17: Favo Carr   **231**

Chapter 18: Always in Motion   **247**

Chapter 19: The Mundaline   **253**

Chapter 20: Finding Allies Among the Dead   **269**

Chapter 21: Answers and Questions   **285**

Prologue

Aerthos, majestic sphere of elemental life and wonders, burst forth from the womb as a babe, blind and singing. She arrived filled with the void and seeking to be filled. The song was given form, and the form was given life. Life spread across the face of the void, and the void was flung from its silent reverie to chase after starlight and desolation.

One small star shifted from its nest and led the void in pursuit to the end of time; in its wake it left the twin moons, Grindel and Prama, brother and sister to Aerthos, to care for the young babe.

The babe sang out, and its song sundered the silence as if light and darkness; the sunlight carried the melodies of Joy and Desire; the night mingled with the harmonies of Dreams and Envy. In return, Grindel gave unto the babe the gift of Knowledge, and Prama gifted the blessings of Belief.

The emotion of Anger attended the birth of Aerthos, and asked, "Unto whom shall I cleave? For both day and night have been given gifts, and what of I?"

But Aerthos could not answer, for she was yet a babe; the sun was busied in its resplendent finery, while Grindel and Prama quarreled over who gave and received the better gifts. Anger in its sorrow crept down into the swaddling of the newborn, warming the child, forgotten and ignored.

And so the life upon the face of Aerthos grew and prospered, being fed by her two gifts like trees bearing fruit. Of the trees of Belief came the fruit of the Arts, filled with the sweetest remembrances of her Song, luscious and pure to the taste; but the trees of knowledge bore fruit with no Song, and it was dulled and grey.

Chapter 1, Tome of Aquos

Chapter 1: Rom

Rom leaned close, hugging her friend. "Count to a thousand. If I'm not back by then, run home." Rain pelted the tattered umbrella just loudly enough to mask the chattering of the two girls' teeth; Rom wiped away a clump of her unnaturally white hair from her face so she could look directly into her friend's eyes. Finally, Kari's head bobbed in as much as shiver as a nod. Leaving before either one of them could talk her out of it, Rom pressed the umbrella into Kari's hands and vaulted the fence into the unknown beyond. She didn't like the idea of leaving Kari there, but they needed to move fast if they didn't want to be late, and the rainfall was slowing them down. Plus, Rom reminded herself for the forty-seventh time, there were monsters out here past the fields.

Facing a choice between slow caution and fast defensiveness, Rom chose the latter. The orphanage's standard issue long dress and jacket protected her against the hundred small whips of the thorns and sharp leaves as she first began to make her way through the plants. After only a few moments of it, she grew annoyed with the many slight stings and pushed off from the ground, using her unnatural degree of skill to cover ten, twenty, as much as thirty meters in a leap. She was never able to really push herself like this: the rooms at the orphanage were small, and the tiny courtyard used for their afternoon constitutional was only barely big enough for the children's daily game of "try to hit ratgirl before she gets away". Plus, Rom didn't like to jump as far as she knew she could, if any of the other children were around to make fun of her. Her hair was unique enough; no reason to give them any other excuse to tease. For a few moments like this, it felt like flying. They said that there were animals out in the Wild that could fly too, far from Oldtown-Against-The-Wall, where the sort of thing like being different could get you punished; but flying was said to be a "challenge to the Wall itself", and was a crime listed among the worst of them.

Five hundred meters out, a distant lightning flash lit up the area near the landmark drawn on the map they'd been given – the wrecked remains of one of the large Machines, left partially-submerged in the ground. She'd seen drawings of them in the daily class sessions, and a few of the larger and simpler constructs were still left rusting around the edges of the fields, but this was the first time she'd seen one of the latter generations of them with her own eyes. *They probably looked less unsettling in the daylight,* she told herself. *Or when it wasn't raining. Or both.*

The actual constructs which had been built to tend to the fields had been simple – designed for the functions they required. Thus they were boxy, blatantly mechanical things – but when the constructs began to make their own machines, their designs took on a much more organic look. They had never known why the Machines began building new Machines, much less why they had built them so unrestrained by the tenets of apparent efficiency; but one thing was certain. When the Machines began to create other Machines, they made them look like *people.*

All the historical lessons the matrons had taught her came back to her with that single strike of lightning as she looked upon what could only be described as a face – albeit one which had to be ten meters in height – half-submerged in the dirt and dramatically overgrown with the brush and plant life left unattended and wild this far out beyond the fence line. As her eyes readjusted to the darkness, she could make out the darker shadows of what must be a shoulder, an arm, and so on. The Machine had to have stood more than ten times as tall as she was, she decided. She shivered, but was pretty sure it wasn't from the rain. She wished Kari were there to see it: this was old Science, and there were few things her friend loved more than that.

Her eyes caught a smaller patch of darkness near the face, a slight movement, roughly boy-shaped.

"Cousins?" she yelled. "Is that you?" Rom growled, spitting out a mouthful of rainwater. With the rain crashing down on the metal shell of the ruined Machine, there could be someone yelling right into her face and she probably wouldn't hear it.

She took a half-step closer when there was a great commotion from behind her; it registered only briefly what a wonder it was that she could hear it, but a growing ache in her stomach seemed to be accompanied by a strange enhancement of all her senses, as if time were slowing down. She'd felt this before in the orphanage courtyard; her body seemed to react to certain situations by seeing everything more clearly, more distinctly, making her more aware of everything as it was happening.

And now, in spite of the rain, she could make out three sets of footsteps – one the hurried run of a girl, and the other, two pairs of feet, most definitely not human. Kari's voice rushed at Rom even more quickly than her feet.

"Rom!!! Help!!" her friend screamed, from somewhere still beyond her in the overgrowth.

Rom stood in the center of the clearing, and her eyes looked quickly around her for anything she could use as a defense or a weapon – a rock, a stick, anything – but in the falling rain, all she could see was mud and water, pooling up around and leaking into her tattered boots. Whatever it was out there, Rom hoped it was small enough that she could kick it until it went away.

Cupping her hands to the sides of her mouth, she called to her friend through the darkness. "Over here!"

A moment later, Kari burst through the branches, still clutching the battered umbrella. Right behind her by a scant breath, a large feline creature jumped into the clearing as well. Lightning crashed somewhere far behind the girls, but momentarily coated the clearing in a silvery brightness that gave them both a clear look at what had been chasing Kari. It stood shoulder-to-shoulder with them both, its grey fur matted by the rain, with yellowed horns emerging from just in front of its ears and curling back around to angle slightly outwards past each side of its jaws. Across its back was what looked like a black leather folded shell, extending from just below its neck and down to its long tail. From its belly down, it was coated in mud, and its golden eyes were rimmed in red, and a sickly green foam curled around the corners of its fanged mouth. It reared back at the flash of lightning, but Rom could still see it silhouetted in place when the darkness once more engulfed them all. Though the lightning might have disoriented it, it evidently realized that a second potential prey stood before it, and it paused to adjust for its next attack.

"Get behind me," Rom said. "When I tell you, run to the Machine back there." Her eyes glanced to the umbrella, and, without thinking, took it from Kari's hands. It wasn't much, but it would have to do.

"M-machine?" Kari said, her curiosity threatening to overcome her fear.

"Don't study it; you need to *hide* in it!" Rom hissed. "Please, Kari, just think of this like another game of hide from Milando!" she added, referring to one of the larger bullies also living in the orphanage.

"Hide?" Kari repeated.

"Yes, I need you to wait for me over there while I go box his ears, nothing to worry about."

She could sense, somehow, the creature preparing to make its move. The beast seemed to recognize her confidence and crouched, she thought, preparing to jump at Rom. It was basically predatory, and it saw her as getting in the way of what it wanted to eat.

"Get ready, Kari," she whispered above the sound of the rain. Rom could see, even in the darkness, its back muscles and hind legs shuddering, tensing. The horns would be a problem, she figured, so a strike for the head was out; the ends of the horns would keep her from getting to its throat, and that shell was going to make it impossible to get at from above. It was an impressively made monster; Rom thought that if it wasn't trying right now to kill her, she'd probably think it was brilliant.

She spun the umbrella over in her hand, feeling its balance. The handle might be strong enough to use as a weapon – it was metal with a solid wooden handle, and came to a metal end the length of her hand. Absently, she considered that it was a poor choice to bring out into a lightning storm, but she would hopefully be able to regret that later. *That was one nice thing about regret*, Rom thought, you *can always do it later if you're too busy*.

The creature tensed one last time and pounced. Even before the creature's paws left the ground, Rom was telling Kari to run, even pushing her back with her left hand to make sure she moved. Rom ducked slightly to draw the beast's eyes down and away from her friend, hoping as well to create a smaller target for her much larger opponent.

Time seemed to drag even more – the monster looked like it was jumping almost comically slowly. Rom looked closely; she could somehow perceive the angle of its jump, and knew instinctively that by shifting her weight to the right and rolling down and back across its path, she would avoid its front paws and bring her up in a position to land the first strike. With its weight, claws and teeth as its obvious advantages, she would have to play on its disadvantages – its size and desperation for food meant she might be able to out maneuver it, and hopefully outthink it. The rain, mud and darkness, she hoped, would keep everything else even for them both.

Hopefully.

She dove under the angle of its jump and stabbed upwards as it passed harmlessly past her, feeling a warm streak of its blood spray across her face and arms. It let out a loud cry and hit the ground unsteadily. Instantly, she felt a pang of remorse. It wasn't the beast's fault it was attacking her and Kari. It was just trying to get food, and…

"You've got babies!" Rom breathed. "Oh no."

The animal was between her and Kari, and she could see Kari making her way quickly to the machine's head. But the creature must have decided that Kari would make a less difficult catch. It quickly spun away from Rom and was after Kari in a heartbeat.

"No!" Rom yelled, leaping up after the creature. "Run, Kari!" she screamed.

She landed on the animal's back, just above the shell and behind the horns. She grabbed on to one of the horns with her right hand to both secure herself and to try to somehow steer the cat from her friend. The animal stopped running, and turned its attention on trying to rid itself of this unwanted rider. It leapt backwards in a completely circular flip, Rom somehow managing to keep herself from falling off. It spun its head from side to side, raking the girl's legs with its horns.

But then, with a snarl, it opened what Rom had mistakenly believed to be the shell on its back – and two great leathern wings unfurled. Before Rom could jump free, the cat leapt into the air, and they flew up into the night sky. She dropped the parasol so she could hold onto the horns with both hands, and gripped the cat tightly above the shoulder blades with her legs. Higher, higher, they flew, up towards the clouds themselves.

Below her, she could see the distant blue glow of the town's defensive barrier, mirrored by flowing sheets of lightning in the clouds above. She could feel the creature's panic and fear – it wanted to run, but it was conflicted by a need to acquire food for its young. Rom clung to the creature, however, hoping they would soon descend to a low enough altitude that she might safely drop off without injury, but they continued to ascend higher and higher. The rain crashed against her, a sensation washed away by a single thought: *I'm flying.*

The momentary exhilaration lasted only thus; replaced by the realization that it was not so much flying as it was riding; but for a sudden jolt and the ground would break her into small pieces.

She frowned, blinking against the falling rain. "Hang it," she grumbled.

Just as she thought her situation couldn't get any worse, a light – brighter than any she had ever before seen – filled her vision with a thunderclap that stopped her heart and burst her ears.

Distantly, she felt as if she was falling, slowly, insubstantial like a snowflake, drifting down towards the far away ground; helpless on the winter breeze.

Chapter 2: Boots and Bullies

Cold, hard tiles. She'd seen these far more than she'd liked, with as many times as she'd been given the opportunity to scrub them clean as a punishment for this or that. But at the moment, they were closer to her face than she would have liked.

Rom's fingertips slowly curled under her palms as she lay face down on the foyer floor of the orphanage. Her hands still tingled from their sharp impact with the stone tiles. She blinked hard, swallowing the shock of her fall. It hadn't been hard, it was certainly more embarrassing than anything, but she bit her lip against the ache she could already feel from the shoulder that had taken the brunt of it. It took her a moment to get her bearings, however. Did she hit her head? Everything was fuzzy; hadn't it just been raining? But that didn't make sense, she told herself. She was in the orphanage: *it doesn't rain inside buildings, crazyhead. Not even in buildings this old.*

The pattern of the polished stone all but filled her range of vision. Beyond that, she could hear the other children shuffling about, indecipherable murmurs indicating that though they didn't share any amusement at her being pushed down, they weren't exactly standing up to defend her. She sighed. *Oh, that's right. Standing in line for breakfast. Getting pushed onto my face. How else would a day start but like this?*

She rolled up into a sitting position, and pulled her foot closer in to look at the bootlaces. The boots and laces were much too large for her small feet, but she'd claimed them a couple years earlier because of the metal plates on the toes and heels. They were designed for workers in the metalworks to protect their feet against sparks and the occasional loose piece of equipment, but she just thought they looked tough. Unfortunately, her tiny feet were barely enough to hold them on, so she'd asked the Matrons of the orphanage for longer laces to wrap around the tops of the boots and keep her feet more or less secure. The laces mostly held, but they always seemed to come undone at the worst times.

As she wound the laces back, she glanced up at the children around her. It was nearly time for the morning meal, so nearly all the children were down here. The Matrons made them line up in the anteroom and wait for the common room to be opened so they could go in and get their food. But they all swirled around Rom, no one daring to make eye contact with the curious white-haired girl with the large boots and the unnaturally blue eyes. But she knew it wouldn't have been one of the other children to push her over while she had been trying to reach down and tie her boots a few moments earlier; there was really only one other child who consistently sought out opportunities to make her life difficult. Well, Milando and whatever Reaper-spawned demon of Aerthos that decided to put her in an Orphanage as soon as she was big enough to walk.

Milando was only thirteen, but gifted with a shockingly unfair growth spurt that helped him tower over the other children. Combined with his four cohorts of varying sizes and shapes, Milando was the only real force to be reckoned with in this old converted temple, aside from the Matrons themselves, and he knew it.

Even though Rom hadn't seen him push her, she knew well enough that either he or one of his friends had done it. They were all affecting demeanors of casual amusement, as if one of them had just said something particularly funny; but of course none of them would have any reason to suffer the pangs of a guilty conscience.

As Rom finished with her laces, Milando glanced down at her. "Aw, did you get hurt, *Ratgirl?*"

She looked up long enough to reply with a casual smile and a nod, and then slowly got to her feet. She smoothed out her faded grey dress that marked her for a child of the Matron-run orphanage. Although Rom's grey dress had been initially exactly identical to the dresses all the other foundling girls wore, hers had been patched up and repaired much more than average. The dresses made for the older, taller girls were made with more durable fabric than those made for the girls in Rom's relative age group, but in order to keep her from going through a dress every other week, she was forced to wear one several sizes too large, with a thick black belt to keep it cinched at her waist. Adding to that, her choice of boots made for a comical enough image, one which Rom was more than willing to aggressively defend. And, as it happened, she did so often.

She's already gotten in trouble with the Matrons four times this week, however; once more before the Lastday penance and they'd start revoking privileges, such as running errands to the market or being given extra time in the courtyard. If possible, she would rather this not turn into a fight.

After a long, calming breath through her nose, she smiled again at Milando and doubled up her fists. Instinctively, his four accomplices took a step back. The other children stopped milling about and turned back to the storm brewing in their midst.

It was far from the first time these two had squared off, and both had come out their fair share of times the victor. But Rom was clearly the more confident this morning.

She drew back one small fist as Milando, too late realizing he wasn't prepared for a fight, preemptively winced in pain, raising his arms to protect his freckled face.

The outcome would have to wait, however, because at that moment, Matron Suvanna pushed open the double doors from the common room, managing to clunk more than one unprepared child on the back of the head in the process.

"Give way," she screeched with her usual harsh voice. Rom didn't bother trying to think of another tone Matron Suvanna's voice had; if there were one, she'd never heard it. "Give way, I said!" She saw one of the children's faces pinched up in discomfort and pulled him through the doorway by his shoulder. "Weren't paying attention, I see. Well, go on in and get your food, now, come along." The Matron was tall and thin, like the branches of a winter's tree, and looked like her hair was pulled back too tightly beneath her wimple. Deep shadows enshrouded her eyes, and the maze of thin wrinkles reminded Rom of the crackling paint on the walls of the supply closet in the basement.

Milando took the opportunity to shoulder past Rom on his way in with the throng of other children into the next room, nearly pushing her back onto the floor. She righted herself with a growl and would have probably climbed onto his back right then had her friend Kari not showed up.

"Rom!" she called out in her enthusiastic and melodic voice. "There you are!"

Although all the girls in the orphanage wore the same simple button-down dresses, Kari was one of the few who actually seemed comfortable in them, if not completely oblivious to the uniformity. Rom had seen dresses worn by older women out in the town that were brilliantly dazzling – covered in frilly ribbons and pleats and other things that probably had names which Rom didn't know. This envy Rom kept to herself, a wish she kept secret from all the other children in the orphanage. From all of them, except her friend Kari.

Kari had only arrived in the orphanage a few years before, and the two had become instant friends. Kari's mother had at last succumbed to the same wasting disease which had already taken her father and brother, after an additional full year of suffering. Kari spoke about it in strangely optimistic tones, at peace with the notion that her mother's pain had ended and she could join Kari's father and brother in the spirit world. Having never known her own parents, Rom struggled to imagine how having your family and losing it could be seen in any kind of positive light. But Kari seemed content to focus her familial loss on caring for her friend.

In addition to getting a friend in the orphanage with Kari's arrival, Rom also received a birthday. As the day of her birth had never been known to the Matrons, they were really only able to guess at her age, gauging it by Rom's height and developmental progress. But when Kari arrived, the two were exactly the same height and took to one another so immediately that Rom insisted the two must have been twin sisters, separated at birth. Unwilling to upset the girl, they conceded.

In most ways, the two could not have been more different. Kari's lengthy dark hair was pulled back behind her head with a piece of yarn, while Rom's nearly iridescent white hair was left loose, falling to her shoulders in gentle curls. Kari's naturally darker skin looked almost bronze when standing beside her pale friend. But their differences – in manner and appearance – only seemed to serve to more tightly secure their friendship. In the years since that time, Kari had outgrown Rom by several centimeters, but the traditionally shared birthday held.

Kari gave Rom an appraising glance, and looked past her to see Milando laughing his way towards the serving tables in the common room with his gaggle of apprentice bullies.

"You got in a fight again?" she asked, dreading the answer.

Rom shook her head earnestly. "No…." Her voice trailed off, as she followed Kari's eyes to her hands which were clenched into fists at her side. "Well, almost, but he started it!" she grumbled.

Her ponytail swinging, Kari laughed. "Well, at least you didn't get in trouble this time."

Nodding, Rom sighed. "It's just that Milando, I can't stand him."

"Nobody can," Kari whispered. "But everyone's scared of him."

"Not me," Rom laughed.

"No," Kari agreed, shaking her head with a grin, "not you."

Chapter 3: Beneath the Watchful Sun

They waited in line for their bowls of the morning gruel, which as always was lukewarm and colorless, smelling faintly like the soap used on their clothes with just a bit of salt. A thick chunk of bread with a thin smear of butter was thrust into one side of the bowl, and a cup of water that smelled of lemons rounded out the morning course.

Once all the children had received their food and taken their seats, four of the Matrons came out from the kitchen to lead the *Sunrise Benediction*. Although it had that name, it struck Rom as somewhat strange, as the sun did not fully rise above the orphanage until nearly mid-day.

Oldtown-Against-The-Wall had only a single orphanage for the just over a hundred homeless children who lived there. The town itself numbered more than thirty thousand, but in most cases, parentless children under the apprenticing age of fourteen were taken in by the closest family member or a close and trusted household. In the rare cases when such options were impossible, a temple which had been otherwise abandoned many years before had been dedicated for the protection, care and education of these also otherwise abandoned girls and boys.

Only a pair of buildings separated the back of the orphanage from a wall which towered more than two hundred feet above the tallest buildings in Oldtown-Against-The-Wall – and because of this proximity, the sun which rose to the East did not clear the Wall and shine down into the Orphanage for many hours after bringing its light to the sky. It was an exceptional testament to the construction skills and artisanship of the initial settlers of Oldtown-Against-The-Wall, this temple, and a dim reminder of beliefs rarely discussed on the streets of the town itself. The marble statues and designs dedicated to gods of might and miracles had begun to wear down under the elements, unprotected by the wall from wind or rain or snow, and yet still retained its majestic façade, though chilled by years of dwelling in shadow.

And yet, before each morning meal, the Matrons evoked their sunrise Benediction before the crowd of famished children. Today, it was Matron Mariel's turn to sing the prayer, which was a relief for Kari and Rom. They felt she had the best voice of all the Matrons, in addition to being among the more kindly to them all. Of all the Matrons, Mariel cared the most for the children and they cared the most for her in return. She was the most likely one to look in on them during stormy nights, the one who made certain they all received presents during the Nights of Song celebrations.

The children heard her voice each night as she cast the protective wards on the doors leading into the Orphanage. It was one of the few forms of the Arts practiced by the *Matrons of Aerthos*, despite their being one of the oldest orders of faith. It was sometimes whispered that the Matrons had chosen to remain outside the wall not due to exile, but in service of the lost souls condemned to life beyond the protective embrace of the Royal Family's influence.

Matron Mariel was the shortest of the Matrons who attended to the orphanage, and perhaps that single fact had seemed to create something of a commonality between her and Rom. But it was also her who had been on duty at the front gates the night Rom had arrived, shivering in the rain beneath a battered parasol, barely old enough to stand on her own. It was she who had given the child her name Romany – from the word *Romanilla*, which, in the ancient language of their order, meant *Season of Snow*.

Matron Mariel closed her green eyes and raised her chin, pausing long enough for the assembled children to recognize their responsibility to be silent and give respect to their traditions. She took a soft, deep breath, and lifted her voice in song:

Deeply from the shadow of the night
we faithful cry,
Earnest to the Lords of Aerthos, Air and Sky:
Hear the constancy of hope
which we do in silence shine
Surrendering to the sunrise
in which governance is thine.
> *Slave away in night and day*
> *Do we beneath the watchful sun;*
> *While out of sight in the slumbering night*
> *Lay the fallen, forgotten ones.*
Give heed, oh skies above we pray
all injuries be healed,
Protect us from the deep behind
your armor and your shield.
Cast our weaknesses away,
unto the wild and untamed lands
Until our souls atoned are claimed
within the Shepherd's hands.
> *Breathe and dream over iron and steam*
> *Do we beneath the watchful sun;*
> *While far past night and dreams and sight*
> *Fly the risen, remembered ones.*

Matron Suvanna was the first to open her eyes, hawk-like in her efforts to ensure that no child broke from their reverent postures to steal even a drop of food before the last note had completely faded from the room.

At last, Matron Mariel opened her eyes, extended her arms to the room and smiled. "Please, you may eat."

Needing no further encouragement, the children all dug in, filling the room with the sounds of low conversation and spoons against metal bowls.

While Rom ate, she looked up and briefly made eye contact with Matron Mariel as the Matrons made their way among the tables, softly greeting the children. Mariel smiled before moving on along her way, and Rom's eyes were drawn to a bronze plaque above the doorway that led back out into the rest of the orphanage.

It was very old, nearly as old as the building itself, but it was well maintained and legible in its flowing script in raised letters. Rom shared each meal with that plaque – it was hard not to notice it, as it was the only decorative feature in the room. It read: "*Sheltered be the lost children; may they have life unending and heaven's wings upon their feet.*" She'd read that sign every morning, her eyes habitually drawn to it, but something seemed strangest about it this morning, though try as she might she couldn't put her finger on it.

Rom's eyebrows scrunched up. She could never make sense of that plaque. It sounded like it was supposed to mean something good for orphans, or else it was promising people that gave children a place to stay would be given wings or… Rom shook her head. She'd asked each of the Matrons to explain that plaque and they all gave her different answers. When she pointed this out to them, they just shook their heads and smiled and told her something about how some mysteries were only meant to be understood by certain people.

"You still angry about Milando?" Kari asked, interrupting Rom's ponderings.

She shook her head. "I'm just wondering if I'm ever going to get out of here."

Kari smiled, taking another spoonful of breakfast. "In two years, we'll both be apprenticed, and it'll all be fine," she assured her. "You always worry about that."

"That's because I can't do anything," Rom pouted. "It's fine for you, you're a genius and you're gonna get any apprenticeship you want."

Putting down her spoon, Kari turned to face her friend. "Don't say that, Rom. You're really good at things, too. Like, with animals! You're great with animals!"

Rom looked around nervously to see if anyone was listening, and was relieved to see they weren't. It was common knowledge that Rom had an uncanny knack with all sorts of creatures. Several years ago during a vicious thunderstorm, the Matrons followed an unexpectedly heightened volume of screams coming from the girls' dormitory to find all the girls but one huddled by the beds nearest the door. On her bed on the far side of the room sat an upright Rom, calmly covered in a small pile of sleeping rats.

A year later, she had been returning from the market with a few other children, their hands full with the weekly agricultural donations, when a pair of alley dogs cornered the seven-year old red-haired boy Aidin and his younger brother Kirin. Aidin stepped in front of his brother, but the animals could only smell the salted pork in the smaller boy's packages. With a rustle of fabric, Romany moved between the two boys and the wild beasts, and pointed back into the side street from which the dogs had leapt. Her two small eyebrows furrowed, her lips curled back from her teeth in a feral growl.

"Grrrrr!" she said. "Bad dogs! You go home and leave us alone!" She growled again, as if punctuating her commands. To the other children's amazement, the dogs lowered their tails and ran away without so much as a whimper between them. For a long moment, the children had stared at the increasingly peculiar white-haired girl, whose attention remained fixed on the retreating dogs as they slunk away and out of sight. Satisfied that they were left in peace, she turned back to the other children, and, still ignorant of their unease, triumphantly announced that they could now move on. Confidently, she led the other children back to the orphanage.

Rom sighed, pushing her bowl away and laying her forehead down on the table. "'s'not the same," she mumbled.

Her innate connection to animals marked itself as a prominent skill, but the nature of its revelation to the other children, combined with the uniqueness of her appearance, only served to further alienate her from the rest of the orphanage. In response, she had learned to fight back. Additionally, while visits from prospective adopting families were rare, the few who did pass through the orphanage were less inclined to consider the peculiar white-haired girl who rescued flies from spider webs while apologizing to the spiders.

A chime in the main hall sounded, sending all the children to their feet. Rom stood slowly, suddenly not as enthusiastic about the possibility of meeting Milando and crew in the hall.

Kari placed Rom's bowl in her own, and put the two spoons together. "It's my turn to pick up the room," she nudged Rom. "Wait for me on the stairs," she said, walking off to collect the other forgotten or ignored bowls scattered around the tables.

Nodding to Kari, Rom looked down at her shoes, and noticed that the laces were untied again.

"Stupid boots," she grumbled. She looked down at them as if seeing them for the first time. *Didn't I already tie these,* she thought?

By the time she was done tying them back up, the stairs were mostly cleared out, with no sign of Milando or the others. Kari would be another few minutes, and the Matrons shooed Rom out into the hall.

Life was simple enough for an eleven-year-old orphan in Oldtown. She and the other children were awakened as the sky began to shift to blue, and they were given a short period of time to clean up and get dressed for breakfast. They had morning classes until late in the morning, calisthenics for two hours, ate lunch, and then spent the rest of the afternoon doing chores for or around the orphanage. Following the evening meal, the children had free time, provided they were all ready for bed by the time of the Matrons' evening prayers.

On each of four days per week, the children sat through a single topic for study, but on the fifth day – today – their classes were generally a hodgepodge review of the material they had covered all week: Agriculture, The Trades, Philosophy, and the Arts. On all their minds and driving them all to succeed was the promise of apprenticeship.

Apprenticeship for any of the children of Oldtown-Against-The-Wall meant leaving their homes to study either with the Professors in one of the colleges or with a craftsman in their shop. For children who already had been raised in a home of their own, it meant taking a step towards adulthood and their life's work. But for the children who had no home or family, it meant so much more; it meant letting go of the hope of a family's welcome and replacing it with the power to affect their own destiny. It meant, in a sense, freedom.

Rom paused on the mid-floor landing of the stairway to look out the enormous windows onto Oldtown. It was a high enough vantage point that she could nearly see the western mountains above many of the single-story buildings nearby. The taller buildings several streets over eventually blocked the view, but it was the best she had. She leaned close to the glass – so close that she could almost pretend the building had faded away, leaving her alone to fly among the buildings, leaping across the billows of steam that rose in irregular columns across the dimly-lit silhouette of the skyline. For a few moments, she wasn't a forgotten orphan in a facility that the rest of the town was more than willing to turn their collective backs on. She was something more; something graceful, like the angelic *Shepherds* the Matrons spoke of in their religious teachings. *Flying*, she thought. *Flying meant something too, didn't it? A low rumble seemed to sound in the distance. Thunder? In a clear sky?*

Classes were held in the larger rooms on the second floor of the main building; the dormitories were one floor above that, leaving the downstairs rooms for visitors and for the dining hall. To the south, the courtyard separated the main building and the chapel, where their weekly services were held. Whatever purpose the courtyard had once held, the large grassy area was now employed as recreational space where the children could run and play with a reduced fear of injury.

Visible through the windows which lined the stairway, the grass looked brilliant green and soft – a marked contrast to the stone statues which lined the walkways along its perimeter. Romany's eyes flashed briefly to the columns and statuary on interior wall of the courtyard. She wondered what kind of gods the people had prayed to, when this was all a temple, and before homeless children came to live here. Were they powerful gods, with their swords and shields and fantastic armor and gowns? Although the Matrons practiced their faith more out of a traditional sense of reverence to the ways of their ancestors, it no longer carried substantial weight among the people of Oldtown. Few things could make them leave the fields for a full day, especially not when there was a harvest to produce.

For the enduring people of Oldtown-Against-The-Wall, tradition generally provided more comfort than miracles. As a saying among the smiths went, *"Hope don't fill the pipes."*

Eventually, Kari joined her on the stairs, wiping her hands on the sides of her dress. Rom looked at her, smiling. Kari took her by the arm and the two girls traipsed up the stairs to attend their classes. The thunder was gone now, replaced by the oddly happy feelings inspired by familiarity and thoughts of her best friend.

Chapter 4: The Most Important Thing

Routine is the key to a smoothly-running system; this was a philosophy taught by the scientists in the colleges, and one enthusiastically embraced by the Matrons in the orphanage as well. The structure was simple enough to be retained by the children from nearly the time they were able to dress themselves, requiring a substantially diminished need for supervision. This was crucial for the Matrons, as their numbers were dwindling steadily.

Where this building had once been a fully-staffed and busy center for the faithful in generations past, there were now less than a half-dozen ordained Matrons to care for the grounds and administer in the rituals and ceremonies of the old religion. It was just one more example of the mutually beneficial arrangement of having the children cared for in this place. In the mornings the children would have several hours of educational instruction, followed by a pair of hours of recreation in the central courtyard, and, after their midday meal, they would spend the rest of their day cleaning and caring for the spacious and venerable building.

The Matrons seemed to attend to their care of the children in the same manner in which they cared for the old faith: with attention to ritual and repetition and with a preference for detached impersonality and efficiency over affection and empathy. Clearly, there were exceptions, but for the most part the children quickly learned the daily schedule and followed it without question.

Kari pulled Rom along with her up the stairs, her friend only offering mild resistance. When they reached the landing, her hold on Rom's arm changed from her general cheerfulness to nearly painful enthusiasm.

Wincing momentarily at her friend's grip, Rom looked ahead of them into the opened door of their classroom and rolled her eyes. Behind the makeshift desk she could see a tall man wearing a light grey smock, with hair that reminded Rom of the thick dark shocks of corn in the fields at harvest time. It looked as if he was constantly upside-down in the way his hair stood straight up, like every hair was struggling to reach the sky. Some of the other children had even teased him for this, which had always resulted in his half-hearted effort to run his fingers through it – an action which lasted only until he was distracted by some other fact or theory he wanted to share with the class.

His name was Professor Theremin, a scientist from the college of Atmology. Known colloquially as "Steamsmen", they dedicated themselves to the development and maintenance of the primary technology of Oldtown, from the network of high-pressure vapors that powered the town's various neighborhood generators as well as provided heat in the cooler months to the individual motor-driven systems used to make their lives more efficient.

Though considered by many to be ancillary to the more common basics of magic that protected and cared for them all, the degree to which science had kept the culture of Oldtown functioning and operational could not be denied. And though it seemed to challenge the esoteric nature of magic, the Matrons showed their tolerance for science by allowing weekly classes to be delivered to the children by various representatives from the different schools of thought. The schools responded by using this arrangement as an opportunity to recruit potential initiates into their ranks.

Rom endured them all with the same amount of excitement she reserved for cleaning the lavatories, but Kari had enough for both of them. Of all the schools represented in their weekly classes, however, Kari enjoyed Atmology – the study of water vapor – the most. Or, Rom supposed, it might have something to do with Professor Theremin himself.

Rom groaned. "*This* is why you're in such a good mood," she said.

Kari didn't need to answer – her excited grin was more than sufficient.

The professor was examining a large wooden box which sat in the middle of his desk, distractedly greeting the children as they walked past. The box was thickly coated in a dark varnish, and held together at the corners with brass fittings. As they walked past the table, Rom could see a series of circular dials embedded what she assumed was the front of the box, encased in glass.

Kari attempted to place her satchel on one of the desks in the front of the room, but Rom passed her and pulled her towards the back of the room by the collar of her grey dress.

"Good morning, Profess - - - uurk!" she choked a bit on the last syllable and was forced to follow Rom rather than struggle for air.

"But I – uuurk!" she protested.

Rom's only response was to pull her more urgently. Kari was forced to grab her bag and move along, certain her friend would just as likely drag her unconscious body along the grey wood floor. Kari blushed an apology to the Professor as they walked to their usual seats at the table near the back of the room. Each table sat four children comfortably, but, as always, Rom and Kari were left to sit at theirs alone.

"This is why the others think you're weird," Rom chided in a whisper. "Nobody likes Science class but *you*."

Kari rolled her eyes. "I'm not the *only* one who likes Science class," she said defensively. She wasn't entirely sure she believed it herself, though. "But they think I'm weird because of *my weird friend*," she teased, elbowing her friend lightly.

The two girls laughed, taking their seats. Kari laid her shoulder bag at her feet and pulled out a small wooden box, which she laid on the table in front of her next to the clean piece of slate. She opened the box, and, after inspecting each one, selected a piece of chalk and laid it alongside the slate between it and the box, replacing the lid. Romany watched all this with bored fascination – one inevitable fact of Kari was the fastidiousness and repetitive precision with which she did things.

Rom reached into several of the pockets of her dress before she located one of the nubs of chalk she'd been able to find – in a corner beneath her bed – before going downstairs that morning. She'd thought the chalk had been longer before, until she found the other half of it in the same pocket. She held up the two pieces close to her face and found the break. Pressing them both together snugly, she tried to will the pieces to fuse back with the power of her mind. Unfortunately, that sort of thing was *impossible*.

"Oh, your piece of chalk broke," Kari said sadly.

Romany arched an eyebrow. "No, now I have *two* pieces of chalk." She held them both up side by side as if she'd planned it all along. "*Two*."

Kari sighed, reached into her supply box and pulled out a fresh piece of chalk and laid it next to Rom's *two* smaller pieces. Flipping her black ponytail back over her shoulder, she managed to keep from rolling her eyes as her friend growled softly.

Professor Theremin cleared his throat, getting the immediate attention of the children in the room.

"Good morning, children," he began, pausing long enough for the rest of the children to take their seats.

"I realize it has only been a week since my last time with you, but my colleagues in the schools of Spectroscopy and Horography were otherwise detained, giving us another opportunity to delight in our mutual erudition." This was the way with Professor Theremin. His voice – if it stood still for more than a minute – was possessed of a gentle baritone quality which could quite easily put the most hyperactive child to sleep. But once he began speaking – specifically in regards to the many topics he enjoyed – his voice danced around his words like dragonflies in the summer sun. Also, most of his sentences were so long that they took multiple breaths to finish. Rom thought he was crazy. Kari thought he was *wonderful*.

He fumbled about in the pockets of his long coat, searching for and eventually finding his pen resting in its usual place above his left ear. He jotted down a few scratches of notes in his ever-present pad of paper and placed both towards the corner of the desk, then absently retrieved the pen and replaced it behind his ear. Rom and Kari exchanged smiles. It was a habit the Professor had, as ideas and thoughts would randomly occur to him. He often encouraged the children to carry pencils or note-taking items at all times. As he was fond of saying, "being as one is a slave to inspiration, one never knows when the Master will call".

At last, he searched the room for any remaining empty seats, and, finding none, smoothed out the non-existent wrinkles of his waistcoat and adjusted the spectacles perched on the bridge of his nose with his right index finger. To his students, this was more effective than Matron Suvanna's shrill voice or the front hall bell for getting their attention. They all sat up straight in their seats and stopped talking amongst themselves. Rom looked at his hair and continued to think he was insane.

"Thank you," he said. "If we're all ready to begin, I'd like to stray from our regular review session to share something new… and very exciting." His voice trembled a bit at the end, making the words themselves nearly superfluous.

His flamboyant style of discourse contrasted with most of his overall appearance. The long jacket, vest and bow tie matched to his faded brown slacks, and though dust frequented his black leather shoes, attention was obviously given to assure an otherwise glossy shine. But Rom's eyes always returned to that tangle of hair. It made her think of the fields, and the open air, and everything about being outside the suffocating walls of the orphanage. It made her think of anything *but* science.

Kari, on the other hand, was transfixed by these classes. She sat straight in her chair and listened to every word of Theremin's often random tangential topics. Rom looked at her and sighed softly, hunkering down as low as possible in her chair in what she expected to be a futile effort to avoid the professor's gaze. But as he spoke, she found herself moving her lips along with him, as if each word he said had been said before. Her mind usually wandered from his lectures from the start, and it had been a few weeks since he'd been here, so it seemed a curious thing to Rom that she could somehow either recall or predict what he was saying.

He patted the wooden box in front of him gently, bringing the classes' attention to bear on it. "Can anyone tell me what this is?" Rom noticed that his eyes fell to Kari first, but then scanned the rest of the room. Nobody raised their hands; a few – Kari included – shook their heads. Rom nodded once before stopping herself.

Theremin nodded, smiling kindly. "No, I wouldn't expect you would. This is a portable *steamdrive* – an engine powered by a compressed vapor cell – it's quite ingenious, actually, if you look here," he explained, snapping open a latch on the top panel and sliding the faceplate up and away from the box. Setting the plate aside, he gestured into the intricate maze of pipes and gears to a small cylinder positioned in the center of the device. He continued: "You can see the compression cell here – we create these by forcing large amounts of pressurized steam into the decidedly dense dimensions of this small sealed steel cell." He paused, silently repeating the last few words and appearing to be amused by his own accidental alliteration. Looking back up at the room, he seemed to remember where he was and shook his head.

Rom sighed, picking up the new piece of chalk Kari had given her. She looked over to see her friend staring in unfeigned awe at the machine, her hand high in the air. She sighed. *If there's anything Kari loves more than... anything,* Rom thought, *it's this:* **science**. She patently ignored it all while she slowly sharpened the end of her new piece of chalk into a small point against the top of their table, all the while continuing to move her mouth along with his words. It turned into a game, to see if she could move her mouth along even faster than he did.

Theremin smiled and acknowledged Kari's typical enthusiasm with a nod. "We'll have time for questions in a moment," he explained, eliciting a sigh of disappointment from Kari and sighs of relief from a few other children. "First, I want to review some of the basics of Science. Who can list the three *Corners* of Science?"

He turned to the blackboard behind him and sketched a rough triangle before spinning back to the class. A few tentative hands were raised, but none with the alacrity or conviction of Kari's. Half the children who did raise their hands saw Kari's and dropped their hands back to their desks.

Professor Theremin managed to suppress a chuckle as he called on her.

He never required his students to stand – this was a fact that Kari alone disregarded. Practically leaping to her feet, she responded: "Air, water, and soil."

Nodding, he turned to the triangle and drew a pair of horizontal lines beneath the base of the triangle, parallel to the base; then drew a pair of lines outside each additional side of the triangle, again parallel to the respective sides. Finally, on each corner he drew a small circle.

"You should all be familiar with this diagram by now – representing, of course, our world of Aerthos, connected to the moons Grindel and Prama." Pointing to the bottom pair of dashes and to the other two in clockwise order, he repeated Kari's response, tapping once with the chalk with each word: "Air. Water. Soil. Correct! In the old language, *Aertho, Aquos, Terrum. 'Um Aertho respis, par aquos bespis, e dan terrum crescas',*" he quoted. Seeing the children's blank stares, he translated: "Into us is the air breathed, the water is consumed and upon the land we grow." Clearing his throat, he pointed behind himself to the center of the triangle. "And what powers the elements?"

He called on the inexplicably round ten-year-old Timar, who self-consciously responded, "Fire?"

"Also correct! And lastly, what are the three *transforming* states?" He tapped the chalk to the lower left intersection between Soil and Water – several children called out "Oil!" – pointing to the lower right circle between Soil and Air produced the verbal response "Steel!" And as he raised his hand towards the upper circle, Kari burst out "Steam!" causing the class to erupt in small amounts of laughter.

Rom looked up from the small pile of chalk dust she'd been creating and stared blankly at the professor. All eyes were on her, but she resisted the sudden desire to hide beneath her desk or jump out the window. She was uncomfortable enough with all the annoyed expressions the other children turned on their table, but generally felt less awkward when it was Kari's fault.

She let out her remaining breath with a *whoosh*, which caused the chalk dust in front of her to puff up and cause another round of giggles from the class. She sunk lower behind the table and waited for the professor to continue.

A few more children, emboldened by the collaborative energy increasing in the room, added their suggestions – "hammers," "pipes," "tools," but were all silenced by Kari's response of "the *Machines*."

Theremin nodded and took a took a moment before addressing the delicate subject. "Yes, class, even the *Machines* were made by steel – and not just steel, but other metals – wires, pipes and even more complex systems." He turned his attention back to the large apparatus on the desk in front of him. "This device as well, was made by various types of metal, steel included. And…" he took a deep breath before continuing, "I know that many of you have strong feelings about the Machines, about their leaving and the life we have now as a result of it. But steel is only steel, no more and no less." He paused another moment, and added, "You might be surprised to know that this engine here was designed after the technology used to create and operate the *Machines* themselves."

Most of the children responded with soft gasps, but none were as audible as Kari's. Rom reached over and physically pulled Kari back into her chair.

"Certainly," he continued, "the Machines were designed centuries ago by the scientific artisans who lived in Aesirium, long before we were sent out here to live. We may not be able to match their skill or knowledge in Science, but even in the fragments left behind and abandoned by the

Machines, we find clues to the mysteries which helped create this world we live in."

Rom's already diminished attention was drawn to the row of windows facing the street. Something was happening outside; some kind of commotion caused by a lot of loud voices. A few moments later, the loud ringing of the entryway vesper sounded through the building's halls, distracting the Professor's pacing enough to cause him to stammer and flip through his notes nervously.

As he struggled to regain his composure, one of the matrons stepped quickly into the opened doorway.

"A moment, I beg pardon, Professor," she held up a hand for the attention of the class. Her eyes darted across the confused expressions of the children, finally settling on two of the older ones. "Tierna – and you, Josue, please come with me immediately. One of the others will return to collect your supplies."

Tierna and Josue only seemed slightly more confused than the rest of the class, but Rom's mind was already working it out. Josue had been spending much of his work time with the healers, and it was generally assumed he would be apprenticed off to one of the Healing guilds. Tierna, however, worked in the temple behind the main building. She had already taken her acolyte oaths, and was only one year away from being fully anointed as a Matron. Rom considered the circumstances, and decided only one thing could cause the two other children to be summoned away.

"Someone died," she muttered just loud enough for Kari to hear. Seeing Kari's shocked expression, she amended, "or they will soon."

Kari, her eyes wide with concern, whispered back. "Are you sure?"

Rom shrugged. It was a feeling she had sometimes, as if she knew when bad things were going to happen. But not all bad things, only the *most* bad of them all.

One of the children that sat ahead of them overheard and turned around. She didn't bother to keep her voice low. "You're just being weird. They don't bring dead people here, they take them to the guilds." Her name was Senaa, and Rom found her to be perfectly annoying. In her own way, she was worse than Milando – mostly because being a girl meant Senaa shared the same dormitory with her.

Arching a single eyebrow, Rom shook her head. "They bring *some* dead people here."

Instantly, the other girl spun back around and raised her hand. "Professor, Rom's talking about *dead people* again."

Theremin looked up at the class from over his thick distorting glasses, his thin dark brows furrowed together. "Rom, is there – did you have a question you wanted to ask?"

Rom looked uncomfortably to her friend, who only nodded her head towards the Professor.

She sighed. "I was just saying I know why everyone's running around, that's all." She looked back at the surface of the table and brushed off some of the chalk dust. "Just that someone must've died. Perhaps. I suppose."

Senaa raised her hand again, but spoke before Theremin had a chance to speak or even point in her direction. "And I said that they don't bring dead people here." She half-turned her head back towards Rom, adding, "they take them to the *healing guilds*."

The professor tried to disguise his frustrated sigh by scratching his nose and chin. "I think it would be best if we just--" he began.

"They bring dead people here when the monsters kill them!" Rom snapped, and instantly wished she hadn't. A couple of the children stood up and ran from the room. Rom recognized them -

both had ended up here precisely because of the random attacks by the powerful beasts that roamed in the wild past the fields. She opened her mouth, but she couldn't think of a good apology; so she dropped her head to the table, covered herself with her arms and hands and wished she were anywhere else but there in that room. Flying seemed like a very good idea, all of a sudden. Except, it also didn't. That was strange, she thought.

The stifling silence that followed was at last broken by Professor Theremin clearing his throat. "Perhaps we should continue that particular conversation at a... later time," he said softly, the unusually tranquil tone of his voice managing to draw a degree of relaxation to the room. Gathering their collected attention, he smiled warmly. "There, that's much better."

Glancing only briefly at his notes, he spoke again; his voice rose back to a more familiar level. "We were talking about the machines, and the things we can learn from them."

One of the other children raised their hand; Rom held her breath. "The Matrons tell us that the Machines were made by bad science. They say we're better off without them."

Theremin bit his lower lip, his eyes briefly looking towards the empty doorway. He knew well enough about the philosophies taught by the

Matrons' order – "Science without Soul was an insidious disease of society" – and had been blamed for their ancestors being condemned to live a life without the security of the High Monarchy. There were some developing doubts that the truth of their history was as crystalline as their teachings suggested, but he was smart enough to know when some battles needed to be waged in their proper time and place.

"I'm not really suited to debates on philosophy, Nara," he answered her. "But I can assure you that we have Artisans work alongside our Scientists in all actions, so that a portion of *life* always helps guide our minds and hands."

He gave the children a few moments to ponder this before continuing. "Now what about oil? What does it do?"

Another child answered, "It feeds Fire."

Nodding, he redirected the answer: "And what do we call something that feeds Fire?"

"Fuel," came the reply.

"Yes, it is a fuel. It serves only one purpose – to help Fire interact with the other elements. With enough fuel, Fire can turn Terrum and air into large amounts of Steel. And with enough fuel, Fire can turn water and air into….?"

Kari and a few others answered in unison, "Steam."

The professor raised a second lever on the side of the device, which let out a louder hiss as a pocket of white vapor puffed from a vent attached to its top. A series of gears turned in the center of the pipeworks which in turn caused a set of pistons to begin firing. In a few moments, a tinny chorus of faint whistles and chirps emanated from the contraption, each accompanied by small wisps of steam that faded into the air.

"This steamdrive," he said, his voice shivering with excitement, "is just a small example of an engine, however: this would only provide enough resistance to power a mixer or a few street lights and is used primarily for short durations, such as on repairs or in emergencies. A larger engine could light up this entire building, or, larger still, an entire street." He let the engine run for a few more moments before shutting it off. "This small engine can run for about two hours on this one compressed steam cell. Unfortunately, it took quite a bit of fuel in our compression engine to prepare the cell. But even now, we are working on finding ways to make the process more efficient."

Darvis raised his hand again. "Does every engine need fuel?"

The professor nodded. "Good question. In addition to the risks associated with harnessing the heat and volatility of steam, the other main trouble with our steam engines, for example, is that it takes several gallons of fuel to produce enough pressure to make this cell, which in turn can provide enough pressure to make this engine run for only a few hours. If we can only find a source of heat or energy which does not require the processing energy and time that oil requires, we could power a steam engine cleanly, and, in theory, *indefinitely*."

Rom was only distantly aware of the rest of the conversation, still furious about Senaa's attempts to get her into trouble. It wasn't her fault she didn't like these classes – the only thing that made them even remotely interesting was sitting next to Kari and thinking about how to tease her later about how much she loved this sort of thing.

As she continued to spin the piece of chalk in her fingers, it snapped in half. She winced, looking up to see if Kari had noticed.

She had.

Rom held up the two new pieces of chalk and mouthed the word, "Four."

Shaking her head, Kari waited just long enough to get the Professor's attention before asking, "What did the *Machines* use for fuel? No one ever talks about it. But they worked here for a long time, and there aren't any big containers for anything they might have used."

"Now *that* is a very good question, Kari," the professor said. "They used a variety of fuels to power their complex steam engines, but we believe the most common was a sort of compressed form of carbon. Carbon is a fairly simple food for heat – wood, coal, various oils and that sort of thing. We've managed to reproduce most of the physical systems in the Machines, but we haven't yet uncovered the mystery of their source of energy. Our forms of creating the necessary levels of energy are far too destructive to be utilized in the Machines."

Resting his hands on the top of the device in front of him, the Professor's words continued. "But even in our failed efforts to restore power to the few otherwise functional Machines we have, we have learned a good deal. For example, even this creation – a simple, elementary fabrication based on the lessons learned by studying the efficient inner workings of the Machines – is far from the sort employed in the Machines themselves. They worked on a principle which has been lost to time – the science of producing heat – and, thus, steam – without any combustion *whatsoever*. But if we could learn about how they did it…" his expression grew wistful; eager, but with a touch of sadness.

He sighed, seeing no alternative but to cap this particular direction in the conversation by returning to philosophy. "This is one of the things we as *Atmologists* must bear in mind: it is good to create energy, but the dream is to do so and not destroy life in the process. *Life*," he paused for effect, "is the most important thing."

Rom watched Kari scribble that on her slate: *Life = most important thing*. She sighed. She already wished it was time to go outside. Her mind again wandered from rooftop to rooftop, and the Professor thankfully declined to call on her again. It was just like so many of her classes, she thought distantly. They all seemed the same. That was the answer to her mystery, she decided. They all felt the same because they all *were* the same.

Chapter 5: In the Shadow

Rom yawned, stretching her arms above her head as they left the morning classroom. The other children had already flooded the stairwells down to the main floor and the tantalizing combination of fresh air and sunlight beckoned from beyond the double doors facing the interior courtyard. She deliberately restrained the urge to jump over the banister and race them all, instead remaining apace with Kari. She hated getting out to the yard late – by the time they'd get out there, the other children would likely already have paired up into whatever games they were all in the mood for. She thought that if there really was a place they all went when they died, it had better have enough space for her to run and jump.

Firm believers in the idea that shaping the soul started with exercising the body, the Matrons ushered the children each day to a relatively unsupervised period of calisthenics in the courtyard which separated the dormitory area of the Orphanage proper with the chapel to the east. Rom could see the statues which lined the yard gleaming brilliantly in the near-noon sunlight, as well as off the large patch of grass that somehow managed to grow here.

The buildings nearest the Wall were the tallest and generally the most elaborate, and always reminded Rom of Milando and some of his friends – bigger than the rest of the children and using that difference in size to both intimidate the younger and smaller children, as well as attempt to endear themselves to the Matrons, who towered above them all. But because of their height, the buildings left most of the area around them in additional shadow; as if they selfishly stole what little sunlight made its way past the Wall as the sun crossed the sky from all the buildings that might have otherwise wanted it.

Rom looked beside her, suddenly noticing that Kari had paused on the midpoint landing above her. Shaking her head, she walked back up and nudged her friend.

"What? Oh, sorry, Rom," Kari said, her eyes still dancing with intellectual excitement. "It just feels like I'm *never* going to turn fourteen. If only they'd let me apply to the College early."

Sighing, Rom nodded. "I know, I know. And they'd accept you, we both know it. But *whenever* they let you apply, they'll love you and you'll be the best Steamsmith *ever*."

Kari elbowed her. "Stop teasing. I just…" her voice trailed off. She sighed, shaking her head.

"It'll happen," Rom assured her, her smile for the moment absent. "Just don't worry about it."

"Can't help it."

Rom rolled her eyes dramatically. "Well, it's not gonna happen today, so stop fussing."

Kari sighed. "You know, maybe you wouldn't find class so boring if you listened once in a while."

"It's only boring *when* I listen," Rom grinned.

"Well, whatever, but I'm not going to give you any more chalk if you just keep breaking it."

"It's not my fault, my other two pieces needed a partner."

Stopping on the last stair, Kari scrunched her face up in confusion. "A *partner*?"

Rom laughed. "A *dance* partner," she explained.

"You're weird."

"You're weirder," Rom called back over her shoulder. "Come on, it's time to play."

Patting the book in her satchel, Kari shook her head. "You go on, I'm going to read."

Rom stopped and turned back to her friend, arching one pale eyebrow. "You don't have to play or anything, but at least come outside. I always get into trouble when you're not around."

"You get in trouble when I *am* around, too."

"But not as much!"

Kari sighed dramatically. "If I come out, do you promise not to get in a fight with anyone?"

She was about to answer when Rom heard raised voices from through the briefly-opened doors that led to the courtyard. Discarding several promises she was fairly sure she wouldn't be able to keep, she simply said, "I promise not to *start* any fights. Is that okay?"

Shaking her head slightly, Kari re-latched the buckle on her satchel. The pleasant thought of pouring over the pages of her book seemed an unlikely event today, after all, judging by her friend's mood. Resigned, she followed Rom out into the courtyard.

The brightness of the sun reflecting off the twenty-some statues that formed an inner perimeter of the courtyard dazzled them. Combined with the laughter and noises of the children playing over the grass and around the outer pathway that ran along the walls of the orphanage and the chapel, it made a fairly potent impact on their senses. The statues were said to have been brought with the first settlers to Oldtown; left to the elements, their faces were worn and mostly featureless. Most of them held partially-opened hands in inexplicable positions. Rom thought they looked like they were fighting with each other, but Kari didn't think the Matrons would allow statues of warriors to be in their temple. Regardless of their nature or origin, they added a feeling of serenity to the otherwise mostly cold courtyard. The sun only shone directly overhead for a couple hours, but while it did, this area was the warmest and brightest place in the entire structure.

The most commonly-accepted reason for the abandonment of this and other buildings which sat so close to the shadow of the wall was described simply as proximity. "In the shadow" became a common term for the buildings inhabited and utilized by the original exiled former citizens of Aesirium, the city inside the Wall; they spent half their day literally in the shadow cast by the wall until the sun reached its daily zenith. Gradually, people built their homes further and further out until they reached right up to the edges of the agricultural fields themselves less than one mile from the base of the Wall. From there, the houses and other buildings followed the gently curving Wall north and south, remaining less than a half-day's walk from the original center in either direction. With no centralized transportation to speak of, the inhabitants were forced to remain close to resources and each other. But while the buildings closest to the wall were often the oldest and most architecturally sound, they were also the least desirable; the coldest and, essentially, the most depressing.

Every day, however, the Matrons would pause classes for an hour or two to let the children play in the central courtyard and feel the warm sun as it passed directly overhead, before it slowly laid its deepening blanket of shade back upon the building and its occupants.

While Kari looked for an available place to sit down, Rom tried to appear as if she was innocently looking for a game to join. In truth, she was looking for Milando. She had the strong hunch he was going to take out his unresolved aggressive frustrations from earlier that morning on some of the younger children.

Sure enough, she found him at the center of a small conflict; an improvised game of keep away with a pair of nine year olds. One of them was pretty new – she couldn't remember his name – and the other was a boy named Whettle.

Whettle Ardmore was preparing to be a tanner – his late father had been one, too – and he'd managed to fashion a decent ball from scraps he'd come across during his time at the orphanage. It was this ball that Milando and his cronies were gleefully tossing amongst one another, far beyond the reach of Whettle and his friend. Whettle's face was red, causing the many freckles on his otherwise pale face to stand out even more brilliantly.

Kari must have noticed the abrupt change in Rom's posture and placed a cautionary hand on her shoulder. "Wouldn't it be nice to have one day without getting in a fight?" she asked.

Rom looked back over her shoulder and shrugged. "Wouldn't know." Grinning mischievously, she added, "It's too late for today, anyway." The yells grew louder, shifting from fear to pain.

Sighing, Kari let her friend go. "Don't hurt them too much," she said to nobody in particular.

A lot of the other children had begun to spread out in a circle around the developing scene between Milando, Whettle and their respective friends. Some of the children even called out to Milando to stop, but others laughed and cheered. Rom frowned. People were funny, she thought. They'd do things when hiding in large groups that they'd never do on their own, but never the *right* things. She pushed her way through the ring of children and took stock of the situation.

Milando stood in the middle, with his four friends randomly spaced around to toss Whettle's ball between them. Whettle ran in a futile attempt to catch the ball as they threw it, and it looked like Whettle's friend was already too exhausted to keep up with it. If Whettle was too tired, he was driven by more than just a petty stubbornness.

It made sense to Rom. When she'd first come to the Orphanage, all she'd had with her was a battered old parasol and the simple dress she was wearing. She'd kept the parasol for years – slept with it, carried it with her at all times, in fact. Eventually, the Matrons had taken the pitiful, broken corpse of a parasol away and disposed of it. Rom had cried for a month over it. Here in this place, the children had very few possessions to call their own, and what they were able to hold on to meant the world to them.

Eventually, the crowd noticed Rom standing inside the circle with the other seven children and grew silent. Milando turned, holding the ball far above Whettle's head with one hand, and spotted Rom as well.

He looked around, making sure his own gang were well-positioned for the new player in their aggressive little game. Pushing Whettle down,

Milando turned and stood between the smaller boy and Rom. His green eyes flashed a challenge to her.

The white-haired girl stood still for a moment, watching the slowly-moving pattern form between the larger children. She waited just long enough for the perfect opportunity and then took off in a dead sprint, clearing the distance in a pair of seconds and kicking hard against the ground. Her jump took her completely above their heads: it appeared almost as if she was flying, her arms stretched out straight to pluck the ball from Milando's hand. Spinning and twisting to skid to a stop, she faced the boys, holding the unusually heavy ball protectively under her arm.

It took Milando a full moment to realize what she'd just done.

"Can I play?" she grinned at Milando. "Or is this only for stupid people?"

Yelling incoherently, Milando charged her, his arms flailing.

From a deep crouch, she leapt straight into the air, planting one hand on Milando's greasy black hair and vaulted him completely. Unable to slow his momentum, the added pressure of the girl's hand on his head sent him sprawling to the ground. Rom kept the ball tucked underneath her arm as she landed softly, wiping her free hand on the cotton dress.

"Ew," she frowned. "You need a bath."

The bully got quickly – if not dexterously – to his feet and rushed her again. She spun towards him and jumped back – once, twice, three times – each leap covering a half dozen meters and quarter of the distance of the courtyard. Her main focus was not so much to keep Milando away from her, but to make sure his four friends weren't able to surround her. Following his lead, they turned towards her and moved together.

A short burst of noise behind Rom made her turn briefly to see Kerl, one of Milando's crew, being restrained by Aidin and Kirin, two red-haired brothers. He had apparently been trying to sneak up on her from behind, but now struggled with a pair of familiar faces.

"Fair fight?" Aidin asked Kerl, grinning towards Rom. "Maybe you should sit this one out." Aidin, the older of the two brothers, managed to pin the larger boy down while Kirin, the younger, held tightly to the bully's knees.

Rom smiled, and the two brothers nodded back.

The next closest of Milando's gang, an unpleasantly aromatic boy they all called "Pox", took the ball square to the face, dropping him to the ground. Rom caught the rebound while jumping to the left, causing two of the other boys to stumble against each other in their attempts to follow her. She spun on her right heel, popping Milando in the head with the ball, and kicked it as it bounced back towards her, ringing with a satisfactory thwap against the shortest in Milando's group. The ball bounced free to her right, and she somersaulted over it, collecting it mid-flight, and continued in another flip as the remaining boy lunged for her and missed. Landing on her right foot, she spun and flipped again, her left foot striking the boy on the jaw and throwing him backwards onto the ground.

Milando tried to close the gap, but after three quickly successive strikes with the ball, he staggered to his knees, his arms protectively covering his face. "Okay, okay, stop!" he yelled.

Aidin and Kirin released the remaining boy, but he had by this point lost what little will he had to fight the white-haired dervish at Milando's surrender. Rom nodded to him, silently commending him for his intelligence. She walked through the boys towards Whettle, and handed him his ball. As he stared at it with new admiration, she looked back at her handiwork.

"What's in that thing, anyway?" she asked. "Rocks?"

He grinned. "Only ten or twelve small ones. It needed the weight, only now it doesn't bounce so well."

"Hmm." She mused, looking over at Milando and his gang as they got to their feet. "I think it's just fine."

Kari ran to her side at that moment. "Rom, one of the Matrons is coming!"

Rom frowned and turned to look back towards the main building. Matron Kanto was standing in the door to the courtyard, her dark brown eyes scanning the bouncing heads until she locked on Kari and Rom.

"You two – come with me!" she called out over the cacophony. The two girls sighed and obeyed, making their way through the rapidly-dispersing crowd of children.

Rom leaned close to Kari to whisper as they walked. "Am I going to get in trouble every time there's a fight?"

Kari barely managed to hide her smile. "Isn't that what happens already?"

"Shush," Rom pouted.

Matron Kanto was one of the newer Matrons to serve in the Orphanage. Her naturally dark skin stood out among the pale faces of the children, but rather than distancing her from them, seemed to make her realize the poor conditions in which they lived.

Seeing the concerned expressions on the two girls, the Matron's voice softened, "Don't look so worried, you two. The healers need someone to pick up some packages from the market, and Matron Mariel said that you two would be a suitable choice."

Kari's eyebrows scrunched together. "So this isn't about…?"

The Matron cut her off with a quick shake of her head. "I didn't see a thing, though the Gods know that young rascal has had that coming for a while now." She winked, adding, "Not that I or any of the other Matrons would ever condone what I *didn't* see anyone do."

She handed Kari a small scroll wrapped in twine, and a leather pouch that jingled softly when she placed it in Rom's palm. The two girls looked at each other, managing to hide their smiles of excitement. The Matrons liked to give various children chores from time to time, and the menial natures of the tasks aside, they generally meant one thing: freedom to wander around the town unattended. If the Matrons knew how much the opportunity to get outside the orphanage meant to them – or so the children suspected – the Matrons would do all the random tasks themselves.

Through a fog of anticipation, Rom and Kari struggled to pay attention to the details of their assignment.

"...and then come back and deliver the packages to Matron Maritia, who will be expecting you both up in the infirmary. Do you understand?"

The two girls nodded in unison. "Yes, ma'am," they chirped, and ran for the main doors, pausing only to spin back and curtsy a brief thank you before continuing on their way.

The Matron smiled. If the girls only knew, she thought to herself, how happy it made her and the other sisters to see their youthful excitement. The time they spent in Oldtown's only orphanage so seldom enjoyed the sound of optimistic laughter, and the few occurrences it managed to echo through the otherwise saddened halls of the once-dedicated temple to the old gods were like rainbows after a winter storm. Her eyes raised to the temple doors – inside, she knew, prayers and old rites were being performed even now; fervent pleas on behalf of a departing soul.

Before they stepped out of earshot, the Matron called after them with the final reminder, "Remember, girls: indoors by sundown." They waved cheerfully back before stepping out the magically protected doorway. Matron Kanto shook her head softly and went back to her duties, mouthing silent words of prayer to watch over the two girls.

Chapter 6: Cousins

Beyond the Orphanage, the ground between the buildings were cobblestone and mortar; streets wide enough for a dozen adults to walk with their arms outstretched and touch their fingertips. A stark contrast to the crisp echoes within the stone surfaces in their home, the air outside enveloped them in an indistinguishable stew of voices and sounds. The earthen tones as they met the lush red bricks, connected by an endless latticework of copper and grey steel piping captured the sunlight and bent it around them, bathing them both in a golden warm glow.

The thoroughfare near the row of buildings which comprised Oldtown's western market was as mildly crowded as could be expected this time of day. Most of the agricultural staff were tending to the fields, and the rest of the city was buzzing with the normal flow of work; the rhythmic ringing of the anvils announced the productivity of the blacksmiths, the sounds of hammers and saws added a chorus of the construction laborers, and even the more literal harmonies fluttered through the din from the music halls. The weekdays in the orphanage mirrored that of the rest of Oldtown; six days to attend to all the labors of the common soul, two days to rest. It was staggered through various occupations; clearly, emergencies might happen on any given day –but everyone was granted their Twoday to recoup from their efforts. But this was Lastday, and it was the day most of the citizens of Oldtown had to make up for any lost time during the week.

Rom soaked it all in – all the sounds, the completely incoherent noise from a few hundred people all speaking in raised voices – bartering, negotiating, greeting, gossiping. And below the conversational clamor was the ever-present hiss and ping of steam in the pipework latticework; the Orphanage was a much older building, and thus not on the grid; but all the relatively newer buildings and construction zones were 'plugged in' to the source for heat and pliable energy. Something about it all made the rest of the city feel more alive and dynamic, but it also made the Orphanage seem all the more cold and lifeless. The notable transition from that place to here in the heart of the bustle of Oldtown was so dizzying that it took her several moments to realize Kari was no longer walking beside her. She spun around, her eyes finally catching sight of her friend, who stood near an open alleyway, her head cocked and eyes squinting. Rom walked back to her, shaking her head.

"Kari, I almost lost you… again," she began, but Kari held up a hand to silence her.

"Shhh – do you hear that?"

Rom arched an eyebrow and pointed a thumb towards one of the many conduits that crisscrossed the buildings on this side of town. "Um, they're called pipes?"

"No, not that," Kari frowned, her hands waving. "Oh, grrrr," she muttered. "Now I lost it."

"What was it?"

"I don't know, it sounded like people singing, only they weren't people, it was like they were - " her eyes widened and she turned back the way they'd come. "There it is!" And, with that, she ran off.

Rom glanced back briefly towards the market. She shrugged, running after Kari. The market would still be there when they were done…with whatever it was they were doing now.

Kari turned a sharp left at the first building on the right end of the street, and ran headlong into a boy only an inch or two shorter than she was. Her momentum won out, sending them both sprawling to the ground with a pair of yelps.

Rom helped Kari to her feet. "Oh. Cousins," she said to the boy. Again, that strange sense of familiarity twisted itself at the back of Rom's brain. Hadn't this happened already? She shook her head.

Cousins seemed to only halfway acknowledge her presence, rolling back to his feet and grabbing a small shoulder bag that he'd dropped in the collision. Pulling a grey cap down low over his straw-colored hair, he gave one last furtive glance over his shoulder and ran off without a word.

As Kari brushed herself off, Rom looked down the street after the boy. His given name was Ballis, but everyone called him Cousins. Everyone in the town knew him as the boy who knew everyone in the town; this had as much to do with his boundless curiosity and good natured charm as much as it had to do with his grandparents, who were said to be responsible for a good tenth of the adults and, thus an easy third of the children in Oldtown. Everyone either was his cousin or acted enough like it. At the same time, no two people, if questioned, could agree on exactly who his grandparents were, either.

"That's strange," Rom muttered. "He acted like he didn't even know me." Though only a year or two their senior, he'd found his place on the streets as a scrounge, as a competent pair of ears and eyes. Rom had never seen him like this, however.

* * *

If she had to give her best guess, she'd say he was running from something. Her eyes stayed on him until he turned the next corner, then looked back in the direction he'd come.

A few moments later, two people –a man and a woman – came into view through the milling crowds. The woman wore a long jacket with only three buttons fastened and a collar made of a light brown fur. Her eyes were concealed by a pair of thick bronze goggles which matched her smooth skin. Multiple earrings glinted from both ears in the afternoon sun. At first, it looked as if the woman was a fair bit taller than the man, but Rom then saw that he was actually seated on some sort of vehicle with two large wheels.

Fixed between the two wheels was a series of pipes and tanks that reminded Rom of one of Professor Theremin's devices – and small puffs of white steam drifted enthusiastically from the back of the vehicle.

Kari noticed the vehicle too, judging by the little appraising "ooh" which Rom overheard.

The two people appeared to be arguing about something, and when the woman turned back, her jacket spun open enough to reveal a leather belt slung low across her hips.

Rom had only seen a pistol once in a book she'd read, but she had always remembered it.

And that woman, whoever she was, had one. Rom's grip tightened on Kari's wrist.

"Hey, ouch! Rom, let go, you're - - what?" Rom's raised hand cut her off.

"Shhh," she hissed. "We need to go."

She wanted to turn around at that instant, take Kari and fade casually into the crowd of people in the market, but just as she had started shifting weight to turn, the man's eyes locked with hers.

His face seemed both handsome and a little frightening to Rom. From his narrow but firm jaw, his blue eyes peering from beneath tousled sun-bleached hair, to the resolute expression on his lips. A double breasted and elegant waistcoat accented his grey slacks, and a thin gold chain hung beneath his opened collar. Rom felt funny, both nervous and a little scared. Everything got a little quiet, suddenly, as if her head was wrapped up in her pillow and blankets.

Rom tried to speak, but her mouth was too dry and wasn't working right – panic struck her, a cool sweat breaking across her brow. Suddenly, everything seemed to slow down; the people moving past her seemed sharper and more in focus – sounds became hollow, like listening through the end of a long and empty hallway.

Abruptly, there was another man who passed directly in front of her. His long brown hair was pulled back into a thick braid at the base of his head, and his thin, delicate face was accented by an equally elegant beard, neatly trimmed along his jaw line.

He wore a dizzyingly embroidered frock coat which had apparently been repaired several times with dramatically mismatched patches. He had pulled a narrow piece of paper from one of the interior pockets of the jacket; it looked like the cards the Matrons often used to help them with memorization. The paper flashed for a moment, then dissolved in his fingertips. He glanced briefly over his shoulder, towards the man and the woman, and then back to Rom.

"You and your friend must leave – now!" he said. Although there was nothing intimidating about him, his voice carried with it enough intensity that Rom didn't pause to consider his suggestion. Without another word, she ran, dragging a confused Kari with her.

They turned back down the street that led to the market and bolted into the nearest alley. Shushing Kari's protests, Rom sped along, turning again at the first left and practically leaping behind a large stack of wooden crates by the loading dock of Carstin's Mercantile. Kari blinked, looking around her in confusion.

"What's going on, Rom?" Kari whispered, rubbing the arm Rom had nearly pulled from its socket. "What are we doing here?"

"I don't know," Rom said honestly, wrestling for the right words. "I'm just having a really ...*difficult* morning."

"I noticed. What is it?"

But Rom couldn't put her finger on it. "It's just.... It feels like I've seen this all before. It sounds crazy, I know."

Kari nodded. "As crazy as me hearing music that you don't, I guess."

Rom shook her head. "If we're mad, we both have an equal enough share, so maybe that balances it out. But anyway, didn't you see those two, the two who were chasing Cousins? The well-dressed ones?"

"What? No, I didn't... oh, wait, the man with that wheel-thing and the woman?"

Rom nodded, catching her breath. Had Kari not seen the strange man in the long jacket? Had she seen him? It felt strangely muddled in her head – she'd have to figure that out later, she decided. "The woman, she had a gun on her belt."

"A... a gun?" Kari whispered, her eyes widening to saucers. "Are you sure?"

Rom's white curls shook with a nod. "Pretty sure."

A whisper from behind them nearly made them both scream. "Yeah, Molla always carries a gun."

"Hang it, Cousins!" Rom spat. He was holding the door open just a few inches, peeking out at them.

He ignored the venom in her voice. "Come on, you little scamps, get in here before they see us."

From the safety of a small backroom, they kept watch on the alley for several minutes through a crack in the door before feeling it was safe enough to sit down. Kari wrinkled her nose at the smell of salted fish and the assorted jars of variously-colored cooking ingredients. Eventually, Cousins breathed calmly and closed the door, motioning for them to sit on some of the scattered barrels.

"Okay, Cousins," Rom sighed. "What did you do now?"

He rolled his eyes. "And they say small talk is a lost art." Turning to Kari, he extended a hand. "We haven't properly met. I'm Cousins. And you are...?"

Kari looked to her friend first, waiting for an approving nod before accepting the offered hand.

"I'm Hikari, but everyone calls me Kari. You two know each other?"

Rom shrugged. "I used to sneak out a lot, and he helped me out once when I got caught. He knows a lot of people in the town."

"I'm *related* to a lot of people," he said, feigning modesty. "I'm sorry about earlier. I usually try to make a much more pleasant first impression, but…"

"But people were chasing you," Rom said dryly.

Cousins shrugged. "It happens sometimes."

"It happens a lot," she pointed out. "You like trouble, don't you?"

"Said the rain to the river," he quoted.

Kari leaned closer to Rom and whispered, "He talks funny."

"He thinks he's an old man," Rom explained teasingly. "You get used to it."

"If you're fortunate," he smirked. Turning his attention back to Rom, his tone became less playful and much more serious. "Ordinarily, I would defend myself against your blatant besmirching of my reputation, but in this case... I've got a deal in the works, and those two are trying to beat me to the seller. Literally." He glanced around the storage room. "I've got a few places like this around the town, I never know when I'll need to hide out while people's heated moods cool to a reasonable degree."

Kari rubbed her forehead, looking back to Rom. "How long are we going to have to hide here? We have to run that errand for the Matrons."

Cousins' brow furrowed. "I've got a few things to attend to myself, which, sadly, I won't be able to do until Favo and Molla lose my trail."

"What'll they do if they find you?" Rom asked.

"Well, not shoot me, if that's what you're worried about."

"I wasn't," she smirked.

He rolled his eyes. "Nice. No, they're just trying to get their hands on this." Reaching into an interior pocked of his jacket, he pulled out a small wooden box, roughly the size of his palm. It had a pair of brass hinges on the back and a tiny lock on the front latch.

Kari's eyes lit up. "That's it!" she gasped.

"What?" the other two children asked.

She looked at them both, confused. "Can't you hear that?"

Rom searched the room with her eyes. "What, that sound you were talking about earlier? That…singing or whatever?"

Kari nodded. "I can hear it clearly now. It's definitely coming from that box." She leaned closer to it. "What is that?"

"I…" Cousins began, but shook his head. "Okay, I'll tell you."

The two girls leaned closer as Cousins looked around the room to make sure they were alone.

"I don't know." He whispered, winking. Chuckling at his own joke, he added, "I don't ask questions like that. That's the key to how I do business: discretion, ladies. *Discretion is the watchword.*" Seeing their annoyed expression, he clarified. "I do things for people and don't ask questions. Often, that's why they ask me to do business for them a second time." Removing his cap, he ran his fingers through his hair and replaced the cap, adjusting it precisely.

Rom's eyes narrowed. "Did you steal that, Cousins?" she hissed.

Coyly, he pointed upwards, "No, this hat is mine. Got it in a good trade with a fellow works in one of the smithies, needed a better canteen…"

"The box!" Rom added, cuffing him in the shoulder. "Did you steal the box?"

He waved his hands emphatically. "No, no, of course not. Technically, it's not stealing, when you take something from the person who stole it from another. A cousin of mine is a Constable; I can have him explain it to you if you like. I'm simply saying that sometimes people like to have things taken care of without a lot of undue attention or fuss. And whatever this is, my client arranged for it to be purchased and delivered to them safely, securely and anonymously. And by purchased, I mean providing me a generous finder's fee."

"Can't be too anonymous if you've got people chasing you," Kari said.

"Yes, well, that has become a problem. Somehow Favo must have figured out that I've been asked to play the role of courier, and he wants his hands on it. I may not indulge in petty theft, but he has no such qualms. If he's after me, he's not going to be happy until he tracks me down and takes this from me."

His eyes flashed, and Rom had the sinking realization that he'd just had an idea which involved them.

"What?" she asked suspiciously.

He grinned. "I have an idea. Girls," he said, his grin broadening in a way which only served to make them both feel even less comfortable, "I have a deal I'd like to offer you."

Chapter 7: The Deal

By the time they returned to the Orphanage, the courtyard was back in shadow, and the rest of the children had already begun afternoon chores. Rom and Kari delivered the packages to Matron Maritia and quickly ran back up to the top floor dormitories. They had a few minutes before the Matrons would come looking for them and set them on whatever tasks they would be assigned.

The orphanage had two long rooms on the third and highest floor, which were simple and featureless beneath the exposed eaves of the building. Along both walls were rows of simple metal cots, with little tables between each one. The tables served as both a nightstand and a dresser, with two small drawers for each child to put their belongings. But as these were regularly checked through by the Matrons, most of the children found other places to secret away their most valuable things.

Sitting on Rom's bed, Kari pulled the wooden box from one of the pockets of her dress. Rom pulled out the five steel coins Cousins had given them to keep the box safe until next week – an equal share to be given them when they brought the box back to him.

Between them both, five steels were more than they'd ever had, and yet Cousins had treated it like it was straw. He'd promised them that they'd get another five in a week, and all they had to do was keep this box safe until then. *Just keep it safe*, he'd said; this strange, simple-looking box – that made music only Kari could hear. They hid the box and the coins away under a loose plank below Kari's bed, and said very little to each other as they went back downstairs to help with the afternoon chores.

After dinner, the two girls lay in their beds for long after lights out, their thoughts on different elements of the day's activity. Kari listened to the music which still floated out to her ears and her ears alone, learning and memorizing the ethereal notes and progressions of the melodies. Rom thought of those two from the street – Favo and Molla – and wondered why she couldn't get the idea out of her mind that they hadn't seen the last of them. It would be many hours before the two girls finally drifted off to sleep, and even in their dreams, their thoughts – and that strange, wordless music – followed them.

In Rom's dreams, she awakened to see herself lying on her bed, surrounded by Kari and Cousins, and that strange man with the elegant patchwork jacket. Each time, he would look up at her as if she were actually floating above her body. Each night – and sometimes more than once – she would dream this until the strange thin man would merely wave his hand, and the dreams would then move on to lighter things; to dreams of dancing across the rooftops in a lovely black frilly dress with matching lace parasol – a must for all fashionable ladies of high standing.

Over the next few days, Kari had taken to humming strange little tunes even when they weren't in the dormitory. Rom asked her about one of the melodies, and Kari's expression was distracted. "What? Oh, just something... you know." Rom was starting to think they couldn't get rid of the thing soon enough. Other than that, they behaved themselves as well as possible, and Rom even managed to learn a bit in their writing classes. But time seemed to speed even more hurriedly by; it grew more and more difficult to distinguish one moment to the next, as if flipping through the pages of one of their schoolbooks.

On Harvestday, a small package arrived for them, dropped off by one of the local delivery boys and inspected by one of the Matrons. Confident it met with their undefined set of standards, it eventually made its way to Rom and Kari. They took it back upstairs to the dormitory where they could be alone.

Inside it was a small pouch of candies, with an accompanying note which read:

Kari and Rom,
It was a delight to meet you both in passing; please accept these sweets as a token of my gratitude and apologies. You'll want to eat them quick before they melt, but you may keep the bag they came in.

Yours sincerely,
Cousins

As Kari popped one of the candies into her mouth, Rom examined the pouch, certain it had to be some sort of message from Cousins. It was double-layered and made of smooth cloth, not very porous. The pouch was stamped with the "Auran's Confectionaries" design, below which was their handwritten motto: "The Quality Is Outside". She'd been to the confectionary before on an errand for the Matrons, but something about the label was sticking to her mind. Or, not so much the label, but … *the motto.* She scrunched up her face, staring intently at the bag from all angles. But this pouch was different. She'd held it before, eaten these sweets before, as well.

"What're you doing?" Kari mumbled.

"Cousins knows the Matrons check everything we get here, he must be using this to tell us how to bring him the box."

At last, it clicked. "Inside!" Rom said, snapping her fingers. "It's supposed to be 'the quality is *inside*."

Kari nearly choked on the candy she had in her mouth. "Mmmph??"

Rom answered her friend's question by undoing the drawstring and pulling the bag inside out, dumping the rest of the candies onto the bed.

She looked over the cloth, frowning. The inside of the pouch was unmarked, except for the random smudges it had received from the candies. Rom held the bag over her hand as she rubbed the material between her thumb and fingers. It was made of two layers of cloth, and only attached by a seam at the top. She pulled on the centers of both pieces until she held them each outstretched while Kari looked at her, confused. She smiled triumphantly. It had taken her longer to find this the first time. *The first time?*

"This looks funny," Rom said.

Kari swallowed what was left of the piece of candy in her mouth and looked closer. "It's two different colors. Just slightly, but different. And pretty bad sewing, too." She plucked at the simple dress she wore, and sighed wistfully. "I wish I had a pretty dress."

Nodding absently in agreement, Rom held both ends tightly and pulled hard. The fabric gave way, resulting in two pieces of cloth. She held these pieces up for Kari to see.

Her friend shook her head, popping another piece of candy into her mouth. "You just can't *not* break things."

But Rom flipped them over triumphantly to show Kari that there, drawn on one piece of the cloth was a map, simply illustrating the Wall, the Orphanage, and a path outside the town, past the agricultural fields.

On the other piece were written the words: *Harvestday* and *midnight*.

Grinning as she picked up one of the candies and tossed it into her mouth, Rom held out the map to her friend.

"Looks like we'll have to sneak out."

* * *

Kari looked closely at the map. "But... that's outside the barrier, Rom."

Rom nodded. "I've been out once after dark. It's not too bad," she said conspiratorially. In truth, she had been only as far as the closest area of the fields, but it had been on a dare. "And this is just a *bit* past the fields, so we'll be fine." The low rumble of an approaching storm rattled the windows. Both girls sighed.

"It's going to rain," said Rom.

"I don't know, maybe the storm will pass us."

Rom shook her head. "It won't. Trust me."

"I'll go see if I can find some umbrellas," Kari suggested, leaving for the cloak room. Rom looked down at her scuffed black boots. The treads were still thick, but they weren't sealed against water. The directions on the map took them well outside the town, deep through fields likely made into thick mud if that storm decided to break loose.

Rom scowled. "If I get sick, I'm gonna *pound* Cousins." But in her mind, she began to think that getting sick would be the least of what would happen.

They waited as long as they dared, making certain all the other girls in the dormitory were sound asleep before slipping from their beds, shoes in hand. Kari drew out the one umbrella she was able to hide away under the eyes of the matrons, and they crept quietly out the door and down the hall. There was a balcony on the wall facing out towards the street, and they made their way quickly there. The doors on the first floor were alarm-warded against the occasional beast that might manage to press past the magical barricades which followed the border between Oldtown and the agricultural fields, so they would have to avoid that by shimmying down the drainpipes the thirty feet to the ground. The two girls had done this before, but never in the rain.

While Rom slipped on her boots, Kari picked the lock that the Matrons had placed on the windows (she'd fashioned a makeshift key a year ago out of a scrap of iron she'd found) to keep the children from attempting exactly this. Kari pulled open the window and hopped down to get her shoes on, handing off the umbrella. Rom stepped out first, trying to gauge the traction of her boots on the rain-slicked ledge. Holding close to the wall, she side-stepped towards the corner of the building, glancing back occasionally to see her friend following closely and safely behind her. Rom leaned back against the wall, holding out her hand to Kari. Using her friend's hand as an anchor, Kari lowered herself below the ledge and climbed down to the street below. She stood back and held out her hands, caught the umbrella, and stepped back under the protection of the ledge while Rom swung her legs over.

She'd made it about two feet when her hands slipped on the wet metal, sending her quickly to the ground. Halfway down, however, she managed to shift her weight and draw her feet underneath her. Her legs cushioned the impact easily. Kari stepped out, opened the umbrella, and took a moment to stare down at Rom.

"You're sure you don't know how you can do that?" she asked.

Rom shrugged. "Nothing to tell."

"It's totally weird."

"You keep telling me."

"I mean, I think it's kind of… amazing."

"Uh-huh."

"I mean it."

Rom paused. This was why she hated being different. "We should go."

They huddled beneath the opened umbrella and clung to the shadows as they made their way quickly to the edge of town.

The two were still a block away when they could see countless white sparks as the raindrops passed through the barricade at the street's end. It was a *Motive Wall*, designed to prevent the mindless nocturnal beasts from wandering onto the darkened streets of Oldtown. Each evening, it was engaged by the Defense Guild – whose sole purpose was to keep the peace and maintain law and order among the people who lived here – and remained up until shortly after sunrise. Due to their proximity to the large wall between them and the central hub of the city, sunrise came upon them slowly. The mountains to the far west gathered up the light from each setting sun, sending dark shadows racing across the open fields to swallow up the town. Enveloped in shadow, only dim lights remained within the town to frighten the beasts away.

The creatures of the wild had begun to invade their home after the machines had vanished, so the *Motive Wall* was created: a powerful warding spell that generated a gentle but insistent shock to anything without a certain degree of sentience. Even the rain passed through with a slight vibration and glowing ripple through the field – from a distance, the shimmering waves resembled curtains of light, arcing and drifting across the otherwise invisible shield.

The downside of this effect, the girls realized, was that the area near the edge of the barricade was almost constantly bathed in a blue iridescence, making them instantly visible to any who might happen to look in their direction. Luck proved to be with them, however – most windows facing outwards looked to be shuttered or covered with thick drapes, likely to allow the townspeople living within to sleep in spite of the lights.

They both gauged the situation, Kari hesitant to continue. Even though the *Motive Wall* was engaged, random members of the Defense Guild would often roam the area on patrol, and if they were caught running about after their curfew...

Kari bit her lip. "We have to go back, Rom," she whispered. "We'll just find Cousins later."

Shaking her head, Rom shifted her grip on the umbrella. "We're already out here; he's probably waiting for us. It's only a few hundred yards out there," she pointed out into the darkness. "And we don't have to be worried about getting lost, cos of this rain – we'll be able to see the town for a mile or two."

"But what if we run into one of the beasts?"

Rom felt a strange tingling sensation between her eyes, and felt lighter, calmer. "Then I'll protect you." Without another word, she took Kari by the wrist and the two girls ran across the half-street and through the protective shield, out into the night.

Before they'd gone very far at all into the fields, they found themselves slogging through mud up to their ankles. It was mostly flatlands, however, and this particular section of field the map led them through was under seasonal rest. Though it meant the girls were not in danger of trampling any of the crops, it also meant the land was unplowed and rough, uneven. In the current downpour, it made for slow going.

Seven hundred meters out, they crossed the agricultural barrier, a simple stone fence line that separated the all relatively even squares of land from the untilled and wild growth. Kari stood on the townward side, hands shivering on the rocks as much from the cold rain as from her growing fears.

"Are you sure about this?" she said, her teeth chattering audibly.

Rom's eyes did not leave the undergrowth. The rain and wind made every leaf and branch shimmer with the ambient moonlight, filtered through the clouds. They were over halfway there, but this would be the riskiest part. Between them and their destination, with growth up to their shoulders and higher in parts, there was no telling. And with the tumult of the rain, they wouldn't likely hear anything until it was on top of them.

At the same time, the same weather that hid potential predators from them could conceal their presence as well. Rom didn't know how to answer Kari. She wanted to be rid of this strange musical box; she wanted to hand it off to Cousins and be done with it all. She knew she would be fine, but she couldn't just leave Kari here by herself. The effort of thinking it all through was uncomfortable for her. She would rather just act and leave the big thinking to people like Kari.

Rom weighed all this and more in a moment, and nodded.

"If you want to stay, it's all right. I can move faster on my own."

Kari wanted to respond – she wanted to mirror the unwavering courage she heard in her friend's voice, but the noise and chaos of the rain on the unkempt foliage shattered her resolve. She shrunk to her knees in the relative shelter of the stones.

Rom paused. That odd sensation was back again, the overwhelming sense of familiarity about this. Hadn't she already done this? She was almost sure of it, she could feel it in her bones, now.

"Wait a moment," she said. "Something's wrong."

"What is?" Kari asked.

"This - - this," Rom waved her hand around. "I've already done this."

"You're not making any sense, Rom."

She shook her head. Kari was right, she wasn't making sense. They were carrying a box with some sort of important mysterious something in it to Cousins, who was waiting for him. But then Rom's vision blurred a moment, and not because of the rain.

It was as if she was remembering it; the rain, the box, jumping high over the bushes and trees just beyond this stone wall, and landing in a clearing by the Machine's head. And then a monster; and a brief fight. And then flying into the sky, and…

"Kari, I don't know how to explain this, but…" She looked up as a bolt of lighting sparked across the sky. "I think I might be…dead."

"You're what?"

"Dead," Rom repeated, shaking her head in acknowledgement of how crazy it sounded, even to her. "I don't know how to describe it, I just know it."

Kari opened her mouth to protest, but Rom held up a hand. "I can prove it. I know exactly what's going to happen in the next few minutes; and if I'm wrong, then fine."

"But what if you're right?"

She didn't know exactly what to say to that, so she shrugged. "Then I'll come back and try this again," she supposed. "Stay here," Rom said abruptly, "Count to one thousand, and if I'm not back by then, run home." The words echoed in her ears, and she gave them no opportunity to distract her. Hopping over the stone wall, she jumped as far and as quickly as she could until she skidded to a stop in the clearing. It was all here, just like she remembered it – the rain and mud, the Machine head and the silhouetted form of Cousins.

Exactly as she expected, the creature and Kari raced from the underbrush, but Rom quickly moved Kari to the Machine and turned to face the monster.

"Let's get this over with," she said, dodging its initial attack and the next and so forth, remembering all its motions from their original encounter. Finally, she kicked up and over the creature's horned head, spinning around in the air and landing straight onto its back. The vague sense of echoing recollection drifted away to be replaced by the firm conviction of having done this before – her memories fully extended into all that would happen next, removing all doubt and lack of conviction. Just as the creature had before, it launched them both from the ground and flew up into the heart of the storm.

* * *

As the rumbling of the impending lightning rolled in her ears, Rom merely smiled.

You can't hurt me, storm, she thought, defiantly. *You can't hurt what you've already killed.*

The lightning flashed again, covering her and the beast in spears of white-hot energy. To Rom, however, it merely tickled, and she laughed into the storm until the rain stopped and the emptiness swallowed her.

Chapter 8: The World of Spirits

When Rom opened her eyes, everything was white – pure white, free of shadow or texture. Kari was gone, as well, and even her dress was dry, though dirty still from the spattering mud of the fields.

A soft feminine voice drifted from the nothingness that surrounded her. "Welcome, Romany of Aerthos, Romany of Oldtown-Against-The-Wall."

"Welcome… to where?" she replied, her curiosity overcoming her concern.

"You have surpassed the first of two trials, the Trials of Transition."

"The what of what?"

"The Trials of Transition. The first is the Trial of Loss, which requires you to discover the truth. Have you learned this?"

"That I'm dead? Yes, I guess so. Whatever 'dead' means." Rom looked around her – she assumed she was looking around her, for there was really nothing else to see but her. "This isn't what dead is going to be like, is it?"

"Would you want it to be?" asked the voice.

Rom grimaced. "Oh no. This is really boring." She blushed. "I mean, I'm sorry, it's your home and you probably really like it and all, but...I don't think its for me, really."

The voice laughed kindly. "No, Romany, but you are now in the midst of the second trial, the Trial of Finding."

"Finding?"

"Yes, Finding. Good luck, Romany," the voice seemed encouraging. "We will meet again."

"Wait, what do you mean, 'find'? Find *what*?" Rom's voice sounded strange – there was no echo, no sense that anything at all was out there.

White faded to blue. Not sky blue, and not the color of the deep ice in the middle of the winter months, either. This was a shade found only in the moment the sun slips below the horizon, caught between sunset and starlight. And it was everywhere – it surrounded her, encompassed her. It was – in some strange way – as if she were made of it, entirely. She could hear the screams of her friends, only diffused, like they were above the water and she were somewhere, lost down below the surface.

She wanted to tell them she was okay – or, more appropriately, that she was right here and that she didn't want to leave. But down, down she went, further past the sunset and out through the shimmering stars.

Then, randomly, she could smell… bacon.

Abruptly, she opened her eyes – and following the momentary disorientation and dizziness, she found herself in a small, simple room. The bed she lay on was of crude construction – wooden beams and straw in place of the springs and steel frame of the beds in the orphanage. The air felt different, as well - - it smelled of… cows. And yet, two other things distracted her from the rest of her sensory exploration.

First, her head hurt. Not just a headache, but a very specific point of achiness in the center of her forehead. And second, there was something warm and furry curled against her neck, beneath her chin. She lifted one hand to feel it – it was soft and breathing – with a gently vibrating rasp in its breath that seemed to suggest contentment to her. Whatever it was, it seemed perfectly at ease here with her. She attempted to learn all she could about it with her hands, carefully feeling it without – she hoped – waking it.

It was the size of both her hands with her fingers extended, with a head small enough to fit in one palm. Its two ears rose up and folded down, but had two sharp nubs on its forehead, just above its eyes. Four legs with paws and tiny – but sharp, she noticed – claws, and something on its back, leathery and folded. She gasped. Hadn't she been fighting a larger version of this? Or had she? Had she simply been dreaming it? Craning her head, she cautiously pulled the animal from her neck and examined it better.

It definitely seemed the very sort of thing she'd fought with – its fur was a similarly dark shade – in the warm light of the room, she could see that it was mostly charcoal grey but with white feet – with the long tail and, yes, folded wings. The two nubs on its head would likely grow into horns with the creature's maturity. And how could she imagine fighting something like this? It was so…cute. Why was it here, she wondered? Or, more significantly, why was she here?

Where *was* 'here', anyway?

The smell of food chased that question from her mind. Food was more urgent a concern, she decided. Beneath the sheet of the bed, however, she saw she only wore a simple nightgown – but, across the room, hanging from a nail on the wall, was a dress. On a nearby chair was a pair of socks with a folded set of undergarments, and on the floor beside the chair was a sturdy looking pair of black leather boots. Sturdy, yet somehow still fairly feminine.

Slowly – ever so slowly – she crawled from the bed, careful not to awaken the little creature. Keeping one eye trained on it, she got dressed. Her hands instinctively knew what to do, even though she couldn't remember ever wearing such a lovely dress; it buttoned snugly from the belt to the collar – not one button was missing – and the skirt was bursting with ruffles. The sleeves descended into buttoned cuffs with even more ruffles, and a large bow was inexplicably adorning the back. Only more confusing than the details of the dress was the fact that it somehow fit her perfectly. Was it hers? It seemed new, and strangely out of place in this unfamiliar room.

She was tying the second boot when the small creature on the bed lifted its head and squeaked out a terribly adorable yawn. Its mouth was filled in tiny teeth, but its pink tongue curled up and made Rom smile in spite of herself. Whatever it was, it was very cute.

It looked around the room, spotted her, and hopped from the bed to the floor, crossed to her and nudged her boot. It did this two more times, and then paused to look up at her with a sort of exasperated expression before nudging her again. At last, she leaned forward and picked it up. She placed it on her lap and scratched it behind the ears. It seemed to enjoy this, but then unfolded its wings and leapt up onto her shoulder, careful to avoid hitting her with them as it did so. Its wings were folded back in an instant, and it turned around to curl up on her shoulder. Its paws kneaded her shoulder and it relaxed again. It lifted its head to smell the air and looked towards the door.

"Okay, okay, I can take a hint," she muttered, placing one hand on the animal to steady it as she stood and walked towards the door.

The room beyond the door seemed only slightly larger than the one she'd woken up in – but this was probably due to the quantity of things in it. There was a table, several chairs, cabinets, and a fireplace on the far wall.

At one end of the table, there was a plate of food, a cup with what looked like milk, and a small saucer. Little claws dug into her shoulder.

"Yes, yes, I'm going," she said. The room was otherwise empty of people, but a sudden gnawing in her stomach overrode her sense of etiquette and she promptly sat down at the table and began eating. The creature hopped from her shoulder and began lapping up the small amount of milk in the saucer.

They were almost done when the other door in the room opened. An older woman – judging by the grey in her otherwise black hair – stood silhouetted in the doorway. "Ah, good," she said. "You're both up. I was worried, you'd slept so long."

Rom paused, her mouth open and half-full of the bite she'd been chewing.

The woman laughed. "It's all right, child, I thought you might be up soon, so I had the food ready for you." She closed the door behind her and moved closer, sitting in an empty chair on the opposite side of the table. "Go ahead, eat up, both of you."

Rom swallowed, washing it down with a gulp of the creamy milk. She paused, however, before her next bite. "Where am I?" she asked.

The woman's expression seemed sad for a moment. "Ah," she said. "Most people don't quite figure it out right off."

"Figure what out?"

"I'll explain in a moment, dear." The woman smiled warmly. "Don't you think some introductions are in order?"

Rom's skin darkened. "Oh. I'm er, I'm Rom."

"Nice to meet you, Rom," the woman said. "My name is Tifi. Cera Tifi. But you may call me

Cera. With a 'C'," she added with a pleasant smile.

Her expression made it difficult for Rom to feel badly about her lacking for manners. It wasn't too often she found herself in a situation even remotely similar to this - if ever, she realized.

"And your little friend, there?" Cera asked, gesturing to the little grey creature who had finished the saucer of milk and was cleaning its paws.

"No idea," Rom replied. "He was there when I woke up."

The animal paused long enough to stare at her, then resumed his preening endeavors. Her head throbbed again.

"Are you well, dear?"

Rom waved off her question. "Just a headache," she said. I must've bumped my head when... when I..." her voice trailed off. When she was doing what? It all seemed so fuzzy, now. She couldn't quite wrap her mind around it.

"You could use some fresh air," Cera said.

Rom was about to protest, but she then noticed that she'd managed to clean her plate. She must have been very hungry, she couldn't remember eating so fast since...thoughts of home tried to surface, but fluttered just out of reach like autumn fireflies. Blinking, flickering, then gone.

She nodded. Maybe some fresh air would do her some good. The animal on the table squeaked and leapt onto her shoulder. He did it so casually, just like he always did...*always*?

Her brow furrowed against the ache and confusion as she followed Cera out the main door into the world outside.

It was a rural community – farms, animals in their corrals, orchards and gardens, with seemingly endless fields stretching off into a vast horizon. They stepped out into the hardpacked dirt road, and Rom was delighted to see horses, cows, sheep and pigs – she glanced up over the single-story rooftops and was enchanted at the deep blue of the sky – it went on forever – no wall to block it...

Wall, she wondered? *What wall is that*?

"Yes, Rom?" Cera asked her. "You seem confused."

"Well, there was... something. But it's not there now, and I can't figure out what it was supposed to be."

Cera was looking at her strangely – she finally realized that she wasn't looking at her in the eyes, but that Cera's eyes were actually fixed above

Rom's own – instead looking at something above her eyebrows.

"What?" Rom's hands rose to her forehead, but Cera caught them.

"No, Rom. Don't do that, you'll hurt yourself."

The animal on her shoulder dug his claws into the fabric of the dress, a deep growl curling up from his chest.

"Where is this place, Cera? Where am I?" Something was indeed feeling out of place, like an itch Rom couldn't quite find to scratch.

One of the things that had been bothering her finally clicked into place. In spite of all the animals and farmlands, there were no people here. Only her and Cera.

Thunder boomed in the distance, in spite of the cloudless sky.

Cera looked more annoyed by the thunder than anything. "We have to go, Rom. I have to get you inside, where it's safe."

"Safe from what? Where are we?" she asked again, more insistently now that she realized the woman did not wish to answer.

Thunder shook the ground again. It felt so near – near enough that she should be able to see the lightning – or at least the clouds they sprung from.

Cera grabbed her by the wrist and began to pull her inside. Her face seemed to shift from the kindly woman into something younger and darker – less sparkling lights in the eyes.

"Let go of me!" the creature on her shoulder was a blur of grey as it leapt from her to strike the woman in the face, causing her to let go of Rom in the confusion. The woman's hands began to glow, and she struck the animal hard, sending it rolling back to Rom's feet.

She picked him up with one hand – and realized that her other hand was holding her parasol. She spun it out reflexively, opening it and sending hundreds of sparks flying in all directions as a burst of energy erupted from the woman's fingertips.

Miraculously, the parasol remained intact.

"Run, Rom!" the animal said.

"Wait, what?"

"Run! Back towards those trees – hurry!"

"You can talk??" she screamed above the noise as a second blast struck the opened parasol.

"Later!" he promised. "Now, run!"

She began an awkward backwards run, holding the parasol out as a shield as blast after blast sent trembling vibrations up her arms. Cera began to run towards her, her voice becoming a constant howl of rage.

Rom knew she couldn't turn her back and run at her full speed, but she kicked off strongly from the packed ground and covered some twenty feet in a single leap – but she landed off-balance, rolling to a stop. Her parasol had been wrenched from her grasp and lay too far to collect in time.

Cera slowed her pace, laughing with her hands outstretched, energy visibly arcing between them.

"I've been looking for you for a while, now, child. I knew if I just kept watching the new arrivals, one day you would show up, and I would have you!"

The animal hissed at her – but suddenly turned his head back behind them and gasped. Cera sensed it also, and raised her hands defensively – as a wall of invisible force struck the ground at her feet, sending her and a cloud of dust all the way back past the house Rom had awakened in.

A woman with short blonde hair landed on the ground in front of Rom, facing away from her. "Get her and go!" she barked. "Come back and get me when she's safe!"

The person she was issuing her commands to appeared at Rom's side – a young man not much taller than Rom, but with spiky black hair and skin the color of copper. He lifted Rom to her feet and swung one arm around her waist.

"Forgive my familiarity, miss Romany," he said. "But do hold on to your pet."

"Pet?" it responded, obviously offended.

"My whaaaa - - !" The rest of her response was lost in a rushing of air as the ground – and forests and mountains, and the largest body of water Rom had ever seen – rushed past them in the space of a breath.

In a moment, the movement stopped – just as suddenly as it had begun – and she found herself in the middle of a forested canyon at the base of a large, flat-faced mountain cliff.

"Go on up, Memory is there. She'll make you comfortable while I'm gone," the young man said. "I have to go collect Force." He pointed towards a small but easily recognizable path up through the trees, which seemed to meander its way up the base of the mountain. When Rom looked back at him, however, he was already gone with only a swirl of wind to mark his passing.

"Okay, this day is just getting more and more strange," she whispered.

"Tell me about it," the creature said.

"You're not helping, you know. You speaking isn't normal."

"It isn't?" He shrugged. "It seemed normal to me. Don't all *feranzanthums* speak where you come from?"

"All what?"

He shook his head. "You are *hopeless*," he sighed. Placing one paw on his chest, he repeated. "Feranzanthums. Oh never mind, you don't seem the scholarly set." He paused a moment. "Actually, now that I think of it, I don't think feranzanthums *do* generally have the knack for human speech. So I must be unusual."

"Uh-huh," Rom agreed.

"Oh, ha ha."

Rom lifted him from her shoulder so she could get a better look at him without straining her neck. "So what should I call you? Ferazana-whatever is too big a name."

He frowned in what Rom decided must be a decidedly *feranzanthumous* way. "First, it's *Feranzanthum*," he corrected her. "And secondly, my name is Mulligan Quireelik Orivallus Perithallireiman."

She opened her mouth, but nothing came out. Finally, she responded, "Can I call you *Mully*?"

Mully sighed. "That will do, I suppose." He was already certain that there were going to be some battles he was never going to win with this girl.

Rom smiled and looked back up the trail. "So, Mully, what do you suggest we do?"

Mully looked over her shoulder and back up the trail as well, finally suggesting, "The boy *did* suggest that someone was up there, waiting for us."

"Memory," Rom replied. "You think that's a person or a thing?"

"He did say the yellow-haired woman's name was *Force*. Should things remain consistent, *Memory* could just as easily be another person's name."

Rom agreed with the logic. "Okay then. Let's go."

Chapter 9: Only Mostly Dead

The walk was a gentle grade up flattened stone steps, all positioned in a comfortable pattern for the entire course up the bottom of the mountain. In spite of the current dramatics, Rom was forced to admit that it was quite lovely – it seemed unusual, but the thoughts of things like "usual" were beginning to fade away like the morning fog. And yet, if she'd lived her whole life in this place, why did it all feel so fresh, and so wondrously new?

They turned the last bend into a flattened plateau high enough up to overlook the valley, broad enough to offer sufficient space for fifty people to stand side by side with room to spare. Against the rock wall, dead center, was an unnaturally even hole that deepened into darkness. Leaning against one side of the cave entrance was a slender woman with long flowing light blonde hair, holding a tall staff in one hand.

Rom stopped dead in her tracks at the end of the steps. Nothing about the woman seemed dangerous – unusual, perhaps, and breathtakingly beautiful. Something seemed almost too perfect about her, unrealistically so. But Rom's eyes were drawn to a row of three gems that shone a pale gold across her brow, all but concealed by the gentle curls of her hair. Rather than distracting from the woman's beauty, however, they only seemed to enhance the otherworldly quality she emanated.

The woman extended her hand to Rom. "I see Inertia has collected you successfully," she said. Even her voice was angelic, Rom distantly noted.

"Inertia?"

The woman nodded. "The young man who brought you here. He is called Inertia; his companion is Force, and I am Memory."

Rom felt strangely clumsy and tomboyish in the presence of this woman, and was briefly overcome by a sense of self-consciousness to which she was unaccustomed. And yet, something in how the woman regarded her made her feel more significant, as well. All in all, it was unsettlingly overwhelming.

But one look at the dark patch of shadow behind the woman made Rom pause in the clearing. Cera wasn't, clearly, what she seemed to be – who was to say this woman was any different?

Her head leaned slightly to one side, and her eyes moved from Rom's face to Mully's and she lowered her arm. "No, you are correct," she said quietly. "Let us sit here until Inertia and Force have returned."

With the end of her staff, the woman traced a pair of squares in the thin layer of dirt on the stone and struck the stone gently between the two figures and slowly raised the end of the staff to the height of Rom's knees – as the end of the staff rose, so did the stone within the drawn squares, forming two simple stools from the rock.

"Please, sit," the woman gestured, taking the other rock as her own seat.

"Wow," Mully breathed, echoing Rom's sentiment.

She sat on the makeshift stool and tried not to stare at the woman's staff.

"You have strange names," Rom said without thinking. She instantly felt foolish for the statement, but Memory smiled.

"They are not so much our names as they are our *titles* – they give a certain sense of our responsibilities. Also, they adapt to the language we speak, or the people among whom we live."

Rom was about to ask another question, but a noise behind her startled her - - it was the man and woman – Force and Inertia, appearing in a small cloud of dust. Force leaned heavily on Inertia, her right leg bent at an odd angle.

Force was spouting a seemingly inexhaustible string of words Rom couldn't remember ever having heard in such an emphatic sentence, while Inertia lowered his head apologetically to Rom and Memory.

Memory and Rom stood, Memory dissolving the stone seats with a slight wave of her staff. She stepped to Force's other side, and without another word, the three moved as quickly as they could into the cave. Rom stood alone with Mully for a few moments, looked around her, and, feeling suddenly exposed to whatever nameless dread might still be pursuing her, followed them into the darkness.

The space inside the cave was not at all what she'd expected. There were multiple rooms leading off from a large, main area – which was furnished with a central table and chairs, and comfortable chairs at odd intervals around the perimeter. If it were possible for the fine, elegant furnishings to feel more out of place within a hole in the side of a mountain, Rom couldn't imagine it. And yet, though the structures were polished and delicately ornate, they had a sense about them as if they had been planted and meticulously grown and coaxed into cooperative functionality. Glowing sconces provided a fair amount of light to the room, giving it a warm atmosphere. Even a few artistic elements offered a sense of aesthetic comfort to the place – paintings, sculptures, and several potted plants.

Force was being lowered gently to one of the chairs at the main table, where Memory was taking a closer look at her leg. Their focus was intensely drawn to Force and her injuries, and Rom took advantage of the moment to glance around the room and feel significantly uncomfortable.

"It doesn't look too bad," Memory observed of Force's leg. "Though I'm surprised she managed to do this much damage to you."

"She threw a cow at me." Force winced as Memory adjusted the bones. "And a horse."

Frowning, Inertia said, "She appears to have discovered your reluctance to harm animal life."

"Appears so," Force growled. "Ouch!"

"I am sorry, but I must align the bones first before we mend them. This should do it." She gripped the leg above and below the break and sang a few wordless notes from an eerily beautiful song. Force called out through gritted teeth, but only for an instant.

Rom silently watched the exchange. She felt increasingly less apprehension around these strange people – something in how they interacted seemed familial in nature – and somehow familiar, as well. While they tended to their friend, Rom found a soft couch on the other side of the room. It looked completely out of place, but was soft and inviting.

"There," Memory said, "the bones are set. Inertia, please hold them in place."

The young man nodded. He slowly placed his hands on Force's leg and began to hum softly. The notes didn't seem so much like a song as much as they felt like some sort of language – it was as if she could almost understand him, even though she knew she didn't know what he was saying. He continued this strange song-that-was-not-a-song for more than a full minute, and when he stopped, the notes seemed to float about the room for another breath or two before dissolving into the air.

When he released Force's leg, she cautiously bent her knee, then smiled. "Good as new," she said. She nodded in thanks to the other two, then looked back at Rom. "Now then, to business. Are you ready to fight?"

Rom's mouth opened, but she was too surprised to speak.

The young man they called Inertia smiled and approached her. "Force, be nice. The poor girl's been through a rough few hours."

"*She* has?" Force spat. "Did anyone throw a horse at her?"

Ignoring Force's outburst, he sat next to Rom, giving a conspiratorial smile to her and Mulligan. "Don't mind her, she's just angry she didn't get to stay and fight. Now, Memory tells us you only just arrived here today, yes?"

"Seriously," Rom said, coming back to herself – or at least feeling some familiar sort of mood filling her, "who *are* you people? Where am I? Nobody's telling me anything!"

Inertia looked to Memory, who nodded back to him. He took a slow, deep breath.

"Well," he began, "what is the last thing you remember before you woke up here in this world?"

She bit her lip. It was getting fuzzy, everything that was from before. She knew somehow that she used to remember it well, but it seemed like the longer she was awake, the more distant those memories were becoming. "I was…fighting something, I think. And it was raining – I definitely remember the rain. And… lightning." She shook her head. "It's all vanishing now. I can't remember it."

He placed one hand on her knee, and she didn't pull away. It felt comforting, the contact – like it was helping her to hold on, or something. "It's okay," he explained. "What you're going through is normal, considering the circumstances. But we will help you remember." He pointed a thumb over towards the woman with the long, golden hair. "It's what you might call her specialty."

Rom nodded. "Please – it feels like I'm losing something... something important. Can you help me?"

Force's brows came together above her eyes. "What's wrong with her? She wasn't always like this."

Inertia shushed her. "Artifice found her first, wrapped an illusion around her, like she did to me. It's made the amnesia take hold."

Memory stood and crossed the room towards Rom. "I can help – I can unlock the doors where your memories have gone, but you have to select them; you have to find them. And in the end, you must follow them." The gems in her skin began to glow more brightly, seemed to fill the room. The light filled Rom's field of vision, filled her lungs, covered her skin, and found its way into her mind. The fragments of images she could recall – the rain, the fighting, all the countless details – emerged from the mist and returned with clarity to her mind. All the remaining elements sprang to life within her remembrance – her friends, her life, and all the aspects of her time in Oldtown-Against-The-Wall.

Her eyes sprung open. "Kari!" She stood up, causing Mulligan to dig in his claws lest he fall to the ground. She looked around the room, as if seeing it all for the first time. She had to blink her eyes repeatedly as memories sorted themselves, but Memory held her for balance.

Rom stepped away, determined to stand unassisted on her own feet. At last, she turned to face the other three. "Okay. So where am I and how do I get home?"

Force smiled. "Now I remember why I liked you," she told Rom. "You remind me of me: right to the point."

Memory nodded, and took her seat once more while Inertia rose and took a step closer to Rom.

"Well, *where* you are is a tough question to answer. You're technically still on your home planet, the world we call *Aerthos*." he explained, a bit of struggle apparent in his voice. It was clear to Rom that this was not going to be a simple explanation.

"But you're kind of….well, dead."

"Dead?" Rom's eyebrows furrowed – it actually made her head hurt a bit less to do that, she noticed. "How can I be *kind of* dead?" More memories rushed back, of the loop her mind had been making before she'd appeared here, and the field of white air that had surrounded her. She nodded, allowing the thoughts to struggle to organize themselves.

"Ah, well…" Inertia's mouth remained open for a moment, suddenly unsure of how to continue. "Memory?"

"Your body sustained injuries – through being struck by lightning and then falling from a great height – which would have killed anyone. The shock of these events all but severed the connection between your body and your spirit, which resulted in your spirit" Memory gestured at Rom's form, "appearing here."

"Where is here – Heaven, or something?"

Inertia's chuckle was polite, but still annoyed Rom. She didn't like not knowing something, particularly something which directly involved her – it was the kind of thing that usually irked her when anyone but Kari did it.

"I wouldn't call it that, but it's definitely a world of spirits. Everyone who dies on a world comes to a place like this," he explained. "Unless other provisions are made."

She stared at him for another long moment, and finally turned her gaze away from him towards Memory, satisfied that she, at least, might explain herself.

"Allow me to offer a possible explanation," she said. "There are many worlds, like the one upon which you have lived. And on each of these worlds, there are charged at the least one…caretaker of sorts, who assists each soul on that world to move beyond at the moment of their death. It is their responsibility and their mission, to help them. They are given certain abilities to help them in this assignment, but are left to their own sense of duty as to how this is to be done. Do you understand me so far?"

Rom nodded, and sat back down on the couch.

"These caretakers are called the Sheharid Is'iin – this is the name as they are known among themselves, though they are often called by other names in the people who know of them: Harvesters, Collectors – among my people, they were called Dreamwalkers."

"*Reapers*," Rom breathed.

Memory nodded. "Yes, exactly. We have spoken with many of the people who have come here from your world, and that is the word they have used."

Rom pointed a shaking finger towards Memory. "Are you….a Reaper?"

Extending her hands to include Inertia and Force, Memory nodded in agreement. "We all are," she replied.

Inertia raised his eyebrows towards Memory, who nodded again.

"As are you, Rom."

It took an extra moment to click for her. Her head snapped back towards Memory. "Wait, what?"

"Wouldn't I *know* if I was a Reaper?" Rom asked. "Wouldn't there be some sort of…I don't know, some sign of it? How do you even know I'm one?"

"There are several ways any of us can know," Memory explained. "Usually, there are more than one of the Sheharid Is'iin on every planet – and if or when one falls, they are reborn in a new form. The remaining Is'iin of that world remain vigilant until they have awakened." Memory pointed towards one of the gems on her forehead. "These appear after that moment."

"But I don't have any of those," Rom said.

Memory shook her head in agreement. "Here in this world," she continued, "you stood out like the sun in the sky – your arrival was obvious to all of us, the moment your spirit came to this realm. That is why Artifice found you so quickly."

"Artifice?"

"The woman we rescued you from," Memory explained.

"She said her name was Cera," Rom said, confused. "With a C," she said.

Inertia chuckled. "Her idea of a riddle. She is practiced at the art of deceit, but does so with the pride of one who believes herself too clever for her victims."

Rom frowned. "I don't understand. Why did she want me? What was she going to do to me?"

Force leaned closer, rolling up one of her sleeves to display a deep red gem on the back of her wrist. "These gems are not simply a sign of our calling; we are strengthened by the spirits who pass through them on their way to the realms to come."

Inertia nodded, adding, "So our being here – and *your* being here – strengthens Artifice, since she is the keeper of this gem."

"Which gem?"

Memory tapped the floor with her staff. "This gem – this world of spirits."

Rom stood up, forcing Mulligan again to clutch desperately to her shoulder. "Wait, you're saying we're in some kind of gem?"

"Yes," Memory replied. "In a manner of speaking."

"And it belongs to her – to Artifice?"

Memory nodded again.

"But how can she be inside, too? Don't you have to be…dead?"

"The people of a particular world, yes, come to their *spiritual* world when their spirits leave their bodies, and the gems we possessed in life associate us also to that world. But a Sheharid Is'iin can also send a portion of their spirit into the gem – they also can draw spirits back, or send the spirits forward – they have a strong degree of control over the spirits of those who have been separated from their physical forms. It is the key to the power and responsibilities possessed by all Sheharid Is'iin."

Inertia continued the explanation. "The souls of all people, when they die, come here. But what marks a person as a Sheharid Is'iin is the power to go back. The bond between your soul and your body is stronger than with regular people, but it will weaken the longer you are here. This is why Artifice seeks to delay your return – because if you do not return, she will own your soul, as well."

Rom felt her fists clenching. "So she's got us here?"

Inertia stood and walked closer to Rom, smiling. "Us, yes," he said. "But not you – not yet, anyway." Placing one hand on her head, his thumb rested against the odd knot in her forehead. "Your body is still alive – we can send you back."

Chapter 10: Remembering Life

Inertia explained. "Your body cannot easily be permanently killed. We may have time, while Artifice tries to locate it, to prepare you and show you how to send your soul back. We suspect she will focus more on attempting to find you here in this world – it is the only way she can directly attempt to sever the ties between your soul and your body."

"But if she were to find it there," Rom said, becoming suddenly anxious, "she could kill me...completely?"

Memory nodded. "But do not worry, dear. We have a friend who watches over you even now. He is tending to your wounds and keeping you safe, even as we do here."

Rom blinked – her headache had, in fact, vanished. The pressure that had been pounding on her head was gone, replaced now with an almost dizzying lightness.

The three others were looking at her with surprised but contented smiles on their faces.

"What?"

Inertia looked over his shoulder onto the table, and picked up a flat plate. He handed it over to Rom so she could see her reflection in the shiny surface. She nearly dropped it. Her right hand slowly rose to touch the purplish glowing gem she could now see clearly in the center of her forehead.

"Is that…?"

They nodded. "You are awakening, Rom," Memory explained. "You are very nearly reborn."

"Is that real?" she asked, her eyes widening. "Am I going to have that on my head when I wake up?"

He nodded. "It is the mark of a Sheharid; a declaration to all that you are what you are; and it also serves as a physical connection for you when you live again."

Her mind raced from the constant fights in the orphanage to the creature that had all but killed her and sent her here, to her narrow escape from Artifice. "So what happens now? How do I learn what I can do?"

"That," Memory frowned, "is something we unfortunately no longer have time for. Now that you are awakened, you shine brightly enough that Artifice will be able to find you, even through the concealing magics I have cast. And your newly-awakened mind is too strong for me to teach you the way I would normally do so – through implanting memories in your mind that unlock themselves." Her eyes rested on Mulligan. "However, I have an idea."

She looked at Inertia and Force. "You must awaken her connection to her body – Inertia, remind her muscles how to be as strong as they can be; Force, you must endow her bones with the power to endure Inertia's magic." She extended her arms towards Mulligan, and he leapt to her. "And to you I will give you what wisdom I can impart, little one."

Thunder rolled in the distance. "She's coming," Inertia said. "She's breaking through my outer shields."

Memory scratched Mulligan behind the ears and Rom could again see her gems glowing brightly. "This will not hurt one bit," she said to him. "But you will be quite dizzy and sleepy for the first day or so as the thoughts untangle themselves."

Inertia turned his attention to Rom, and she saw the ground beneath him glow similarly, though more deeply green in color. "Give us your hands," he asked. She did so, and Force and Inertia both held her hands, their gems bursting with visible energy. Her arms throbbed; her skin felt as if it were on fire – but she gritted her teeth and focused on the certainty that it was necessary to both defend herself and, perhaps one day, take the fight back to Artifice for what she had done.

The pain subsided, and they released her hands – Memory was standing before her, and carefully handed Mulligan back. He weakly crawled back up onto her shoulder, and sighed softly before resting his head on his paws, his eyes half-closed.

"Now then, Rom," Memory began, "a newly awakened Is'iin mind closes itself off when it transforms – it's a defensive measure that happens to all of us, like the chrysalis of a butterfly."

"A what?" Rom asked.

Memory ignored the girl's question. "It means your mind is powerfully protected from me, so I cannot send you back to your body by myself – I can only try to teach you how to do it."

The walls and floor shook suddenly and briefly; this was followed by another loud explosion from outside the cave entrance.

Memory looked directly at Rom, but spoke to Inertia. "How much more can you hold her?"

Inertia was supporting himself against a chair, sweat beading up on his face. "Maybe another minute, two or three," he said.

Force picked up her sword and shield. "I'll go buy us some time. Good luck, Rom. You're going to be fine." She bowed her head slightly and turned to leave. "No horses around here now, you crazy bitch!" she called out as she walked outside, brandishing her sword defiantly.

Memory drew Rom's attention back to her. "I'm sorry, but we're going to have to be brief on this – I will do all I can, but most of this will be up to you. Are you ready?"

Rom nodded, even though she didn't even *approach* feeling ready.

"You have to remember who you were. Remember everything about yourself – think about who you are, who you were; think of your friends, your home. You must think of every detail – every smell, every sound, every feeling. This is the thread upon which you must pull yourself back. Do not let go of that thread."

She looked into the woman's eyes, saw the reflection of Memory's golden gems burning brightly into her own eyes. Randomly, Rom thought Memory seemed exceptionally sad, for some reason.

"No! Do not think of me," she said sharply. "Close your eyes. Think of yourself. Think of your life, your world, *your* memories."

Rom did as she was told – she closed her eyes and thought of her life. In the corner of her mind, she could hear the low rumbling of what was obviously Inertia and Force, fighting to defend her – her, a person they'd just met and yet for whom they were willing and prepared to risk their lives. On her shoulder, Mulligan nuzzled her cheek, and lowered his head back to her shoulder – his whiskers were scratchy on her skin, and his breath was hot, coming in short breaths.

She began to feel the room spinning, but she kept her eyes shut tight – her lungs felt sluggish, struggling to catch air. When she at last drew another breath, it felt cold in her chest, her mouth felt dry and her body began to ache. It was dramatically silent – gone were the sounds of combat, the explosions, the screams of defiance.

Cautiously, she opened her eyes – just a sliver at first, and then wider when she realized she was back in the girls' dormitory of the orphanage. She started to sit up, but her body protested – her back and legs were very sore, and her head spun treacherously, sending a warning tremble from her stomach.

Three things jumped to her attention right from the start, however. First, Kari was sitting in a small chair beside her, her head forward, asleep. Second, Rom realized that she was wearing the same clothing she'd been wearing in that spirit world –

the cloth still felt smooth and clean. Third, a warm ball of fur was curled up against her shoulder, snoring softly.

Her mind reeled – she was home again, but the dress and Mulligan were evidence that she had, in fact, been there – and somehow brought them back with her. That left one further detail to verify. In spite of the protests of her aching shoulder, she raised her hand to her forehead. With a soft gasp, she felt the smooth surface of the spirit gem – actually there, firmly embedded in her skin. *It was real?* She thought. *It **was** real.*

Either the movement or her gasp caused Mulligan to rouse, and he arched his neck and yawned deeply, pink tongue curling up at the end. He smacked his lips a couple of times, and stood up. "Where are we?" he whispered.

Rom shushed him softly, pointing her eyes towards the sleeping Kari.

"Oh," he mouthed. "Sorry. Friend of yours?"

"That's my best friend Kari. She must've stayed here to watch over me."

Mully nodded. "Good friend," he agreed.

Kari stirred, her eyes fluttering open. She looked at Rom, then Mulligan, and back to Rom.

Instinctively, she kicked back from the strange animal and tipped backwards over in her chair.

The wood of the chair clattered loudly against the floorboards and mingled with Kari's yelp. Rom swung her legs slowly onto the floor and stepped over to help Kari back to her feet.

"You okay?" she asked.

Kari swept the hair back from her face, smoothed out her dress, and struggled to make sense of the moment. "Am I okay? I'm fine! But - - how - - - what - - what's that on your head?"

Rom looked around the room – it was morning, probably not too long after breakfast, so most of the children were either in class or out playing in the yard. But a Matron could be in here at potentially any moment to check on her.

Self-consciously, Rom mussed her hair to try and conceal the gem on her forehead. "I'll explain, I promise. But first you need to tell me what happened. How long have I been here? How did I get here?"

They both sat back down on their beds, facing one another. Mully crawled up into Rom's lap and allowed her to scratch the back of his head and neck.

"Oh, Rom, it was terrible!" Kari said. "You took off with that monster and you just went up and up, and then there was a big crash and I couldn't see you! Then Cousins saw you fall and we ran over, and…" her eyes welled up. "I thought you were dead. You were burned and your arm and legs were both turned funny… I was so afraid, I thought you were…!"

Rom frowned sympathetically. She'd seen the image of herself, thanks to Memory – she could only imagine how horrible it had to have been for Kari to have seen it up close.

"Cousins had a couple of people there – they were the ones who he was supposed to deliver the box to," she lowered her voice when saying that – "and they helped carry you back inside. They did some kind of medical thing and fixed your arm and legs, but your skin was still really darkly burned. They wrapped you in bandages, and the man – he didn't say his name – carried you back here this morning. The Matrons were so mad, but he pulled Matron Suvanna aside and said something to her and her face was all red but she didn't punish us. And she let me stay up here and watch you, but now…you're all better! And…that dress is really cute!"

"So it all just happened last night?"

Kari nodded, her eyes dropping to Mulligan, who was purring gently. "What's that?"

Rom grinned. "This," she stopped petting the little grey feranzanthum, who growled softly in protest, "is Mulligan. He was…with me, there."

"What do you mean, '*there*'?"

Rom sighed. She didn't quite understand it yet, herself. "I went to someplace else. I found these clothes and met Mulligan and some other people, and they helped me come back here. I guess the clothes and Mully came with me somehow."

"Also, you're not hurt anymore. That's amazing!"

"I don't *feel* not hurt. My body's killing me." She massaged her right shoulder, but strangely enough, it didn't ache very much now. "Hmm. Or maybe not."

She stood up, lifting Mulligan to her shoulder, and took a few steps around the room. With each step, her legs and back felt better and better – after ten steps, she didn't feel any discomfort at all.

Her mind recalled the strange and painful magic Inertia and Force had done – had that helped her somehow heal herself?

When she turned around, she was smiling broadly. Kari was still sitting on the bed, turned to watch what her mind told her was impossible – nevertheless, there was her friend, looking not only as if nothing had happened to her, but dressed in a fine dress, a strange looking animal on her shoulder, and a brightly glowing gem stuck somehow on her forehead.

She was about to ask something more when the far door opened. Rom quickly dropped Mulligan onto her bed, turning and standing in front of him to block him from sight as the Matron entered with Cousins.

They both stopped in their steps, her with a look of confusion on her face, one of curiosity on his.

"Miss Rom!" she said, pushing past Cousins to run towards her. Rom flashed Kari a quick look, and Kari stood and took her place by the bed, maintaining Mully from view as Rom moved to intercept the Matron.

"Matron Mariel," she said, as the Matron wrapped her arms around Rom in a fierce hug.

"We were so worried about you! The other Matrons said you looked terrible, what with all the burns and cuts!" she took Rom in her hands, holding her back far enough to get a fair appraisal of the girl. "Why, you don't look at all harmed," she said, relief apparent in her voice. She embraced Rom once more, then turned to Cousins.

"Well, it looks like I'll have to ask Matron Suvanna to sign those papers over, after all. I'll be sure to have them ready downstairs, whenever you're ready to leave."

He bowed, affecting the sort of demeanor generally held only by the other adults when they interacted – it looked strange when he did it, but if she thought it silly, Matron Mariel did not even crack a smile, aside from politely excusing herself and leaving.

"Papers? What are you up to now, Cousins?" Rom asked him, instantly suspicious.

His serious expression dissolved into a wide smile. "Girls, I'm breaking you out of here. We leave immediately."

"What?" both girls echoed.

"We're *twelve*, Cousins!" Kari said angrily.

"Eleven," corrected Rom. "But almost twelve."

"Okay, almost twelve," Kari conceded. "Either way, we can't be on our own until we're fourteen."

"You're correct," he said. He was annoying when he was smug. And he was smug far too often for Rom's liking.

Rom rolled her eyes. "All right, spill it. What's going on?"

Shrugging, Cousins answered. "You've been adopted. Both of you."

"Adopted?" Kari moved forward, eying him suspiciously as well. "By who?"

"Whom," he responded.

"By *whom*, then?" Kari repeated, taking another threatening step closer to him.

"It's not my place to say," he answered flippantly. "Besides, you wouldn't believe me if I told you." He turned around, tossing an envelope over his shoulder at the girls. "But they did tell me to give you this. It doesn't explain much, though."

He opened the door. "I'll wait for you both downstairs. Don't be too long, I've got other errands to run today."

The two girls continued to stare at the door after he'd closed it behind him.

Kari shook her head, annoyed at how much delight Cousins seemed to be having at their expense. "If you don't hit him, I will."

Rom nodded absently. She was already opening the envelope and pulling out the paper inside. Written in a very elegant hand, it read:

Mss. Rom and Kari,

> *I apologize that this must come so suddenly to you, and under so auspicious of circumstances. However, the luxury of watching you both from afar is no longer an option, and I must bring you closer so that I*

might both prepare and protect you from what is to come.

I am making all the arrangements so that you may both reside in my home, should you be amenable to this, and will ensure that all your needs are met; in exchange for which, I shall see to it that you are both apprenticed into appropriate skills, and, additionally, given the opportunity to see your true talents grow and blossom.

It is known to me that both of you have secrets about you — wondrous secrets, the understanding of which should become a priority for you both and which few other than I could either understand or provide that teaching.

Cousins will bring you to my shop; here you will meet me and you may then decide if you wish to accept this offer.

Sincerely,

Goya Parva, Apothecary

She read the letter a second time, and handed it to Kari while she turned back to look down at Mulligan. He remained sitting on the bed, regarding her curiously.

Kari read the letter and looked back at Rom, her eyes wide. "Is this for real?" she asked.

Rom could only shrug and furrow her brow. After so many years of trying to balance the most intangibly enduring quantity of hope necessary to tolerate her life in the orphanage, she found herself confronted with the possibility of liberation. Still, if the Matrons believed it, then maybe it was really happening. She sighed, shaking her head softly. Rom didn't know how she'd expected this day to be, and now that it was finally here, she was uncertain on how to feel about it.

"Well, Mully, I guess we don't have to worry about whether or not the Matrons were going to let me keep you after all." She smiled. "Do you think this Goya person is all right?"

"Perhaps," he offered, "we should at least meet her and make sure she's not that same lady who tried to keep us in that world of Spirits."

Rom nodded. She'd already thought of that, but aside from considering it, hadn't gone much further – the possibility of being free from this orphanage was just too tempting an opportunity.

"We'll go meet her and see for ourselves."

"I agree," he responded. "Can I help you pack?"

Rom laughed. "This dress and you. I'm packed."

He hopped up on her shoulder and they turned around to see Kari, staring at them both in shock.

"What?" they asked in unison.

Kari pointed at Mully. "He…. Talks?"

Mully shook his head. "What is *wrong* with the animals here? Have none of them any manners at all?"

Rom stuck her tongue out. "It's not like that, *they* just don't talk. They're actually really mean, too," she added thoughtfully. "They attack people – a lot of people have been hurt or killed by them."

Mully frowned. "That's bad. We should find one of them, and ask them why they're doing that."

"That's what got her killed – well, *almost* killed – in the first place!" Kari nearly yelled.

Rom shook her head. "No, I was dead. But," she conceded, "not *completely* dead." She took a look at the horror on Kari's face, and added. "Sorry. I'll explain later. But, anyway, I'm all better, now."

Mully turned back to look at Kari. "I'm not saying we should go *now* – besides, she needs to learn a lot, first. And," he added to Rom, "you won't *believe* all the things you're going to be able to do."

Kari brought a pair of books she'd been given by Professor Theremin, and the few coins given them previously by Cousins, but otherwise, the two girls had precious little else between them in terms of personal possessions. As they walked down the stairs towards the main floor, several of the children watched them pass. In Oldtown-Against-The-Wall, relative poverty was more the norm than financial excess – so it was rare that a family could afford to adopt a child, and the general expectation of the children was that a life in one of the many orphanages would only end when they were old enough or skilled enough to secure an apprenticeship with one of the craftsmen or trades schools in the town. Typically, these apprenticeships were only offered to children in their mid to late teens – but word had already spread that both Rom and Kari were being accepted far younger than was normal. But if any doubted, they took one look at Rom in her new dress and assumed it to be proof that the rumors were true.

There was no great affair made of their leaving – no tearful goodbyes, no promises to speak again soon, none of the anticipated taunting from Milando or his pack of bullies. Rom and Kari tried to look straight ahead and not react to the painful expressions of envy from the other children.

Whatever joy the other children might have felt for the two girls was swallowed up by the despairing realization that they went to fill two spaces now denied the rest of them. Their freedom, effectively, meant a rejection – or at least postponement – of their own.

But in the pair of minutes it took them to descend the stairs, the demeanors of the two girls were transformed from hopeless and common abandoned children into the embodiment of the very dreams possessed by nearly every one of the remaining orphans. Many minutes passed following the reverberating boom of the opening and closing of the main doors before the children's attention could return to their lessons.

Chapter 11: The Apothecary

The only times Rom and Kari had left the orphanage in the past, they were either running errands for the Matrons or breaking curfew – either way, they'd never had the opportunity to simply walk and look around without fearing the inevitable repercussions for their tardiness. But today was special in many countless ways, and they surrendered to the feeling. Today, they saw it now not just as a momentary, fleeting escape from the life in the Wall's shadow – but embracing the unfolding reality that their new lives had led them out into the light.

They took it all in: the sights and sounds of the market with its busied haggling and vendors' urgings to sample this, try that; the rusty smells from the smithy, and the rhythmic clanging of metal on metal; even the discordant attempts at rhythm from several neighboring conservatories with all its young musical students seemed more magical, somehow. They were not merely passing through the town, now. Now, they were a part of it, and they hoped the memories would remain embedded in the fabric of their clothes, intertwine within their hair, and burn themselves into their eyes forever.

Cousins seemed to understand this, and he took a more roundabout path towards their destination; he led them past the markets and past several bakeries – even managed to acquire a handful of sweet breads for the three of them, which they ate while they walked. Other than a brief exchange of thanks, the three continued on in relative silence. Kari and Rom laughed and pointed, generally delighted with everything there was to see and soak in. Eventually, Cousins led them from the market district and into the lesser traveled areas through the crafts neighborhood and into the segments reserved for the sciences.

When the people of Oldtown referred to "sciences", it included a far range of skills: from atmology to zymology, they had carried the knowledge with them from their former home within the wall. Down through the generations of cast out citizens, they passed this wisdom along through a process of apprenticeships; as children were observed to have a certain predilection for one science or art or skill, they were given the opportunity to study under accomplished adults and receive the necessary education to continue in that trade.

The arts included music, design, theater and several fields of esoteric energy evaluation, as well as the three divination philosophies: hydromancy, chronomancy and geomancy. These tended towards a philosophical and abstract approach to understanding and expressing the world, and favored people who followed free-flowing inspiration and had a poetic sense of communication.

The sciences were more structured, based on time-tested and repeatable processes, relying less on the individual interpretation and nebulous processes and more on logic, patterns and pragmatic methodology. The buildings in this area were a definitive reflection on this way of thinking, as well: where the purely esoteric Arts had their buildings designed with as many curves and delicate ornamentations as their foundations could bear, the Sciences' buildings were comprised of straight lines and definitive structures. There appeared to have been an unspoken agreement to design each college to follow the tenets of their philosophy in as holistic a manner as possible, from the first foundation stone to the most recent word spoken in their classrooms.

Of all the colleges, however, the "Steam Labs" took up the largest geographical space, encompassing several blocks' worth of buildings.

At its highest point, it rose a mere three stories – still many feet lower than some of the other buildings, but seemed taller in terms of implied importance: the other buildings in its immediate vicinity seemed diminished through some sort of optical illusion caused by the many pipe-lined minarets and gouts of steam that erupted and faded into the sky above.

The three children passed a small group of men wearing thick protective clothing. Particularly the mitts and boots appeared to be aggressively shielded, and the suits were fitted with compressed and barely transparent goggles, though the cowls were pulled back from their faces, currently. Cousins, seeing the two girls' expressions, stepped close enough for them to hear.

"Those are some of the pipe sentries. They work on the main lines, fixing breaches and tending to the repairs in the active conduits."

Rom thought back on some of the few bits she remembered from Professor Theremin's discussions on the dangers of steam power; she'd felt the heat emanating from even the insulated pipes and some of the faint pressure release clouds at the ends of the line, but couldn't imagine the intensity that built up in the main lines. She looked again at the hardened expressions of the men – they looked like soldiers, she thought.

As they passed one of the workshops, Rom caught the sound of a faint gasp from Kari; the front wall was segmented in a series of square-foot windows, allowing them to see inside while technicians worked within on a structure of pipes and valves easily ten times their size. Several of the windows were blurred by copious amounts of the condensation which generally frequented these labs as they worked to further increase the functional efficiency of steam as a source of their city's power.

"They're not using carbon," Kari said. "It looks like it would be completely smokeless. Either that or they're working on cycling the output back into the processing chambers…"

Rom stopped herself from rolling her eyes. The debate of "steam versus smoke" was a favorite of Kari's – she often went on and on about a perfect science which allowed engines to be powered on pure energy – powering themselves without burning the air. Rom remembered the recent visit by Professor Theremin to their lesson, and how excited he'd been by the recent advances made by the Atmologists.

Cousins paused several feet away, noticing that the two girls had paused to watch the technicians. "Come on, girls. You can come back and watch the *airbrains* later. We're running late."

Rom pulled Kari away from the windows, ignoring the small whine of protest from her friend. Mulligan chuckled lightly on her shoulder. "Don't worry," he whispered. "In a couple of years, she'll be like that with *boys*."

Rom shushed him and they caught up to Cousins, who was pointing towards a small building one block up. Over the main door on the corner of the building, a small hand-painted sign gently swung in the late morning air that read: "Apothecary."

"What's an apothecary?" Rom whispered to Kari.

Kari frowned. "It's a person who stuffs dead animals."

Mully shook his head. "No, that's a *taxidermist*. An *apothecary* deals in potions and chemicals."

"You're right," Cousins called back over his shoulder. He turned around, looking at Rom. "You might want to keep him a bit quieter, by the way. A talking beast like him would catch a lot of money in the right markets." He winked at Mulligan. "Just a friendly bit of advice."

Mully nodded and curled closer into Rom's hair.

Cousins returned the nod and walked them the rest of the way to the door. He held it open for them, letting the small bell ring cheerily as they entered and ring again as the door closed behind them.

Rom had only been here once before; she'd been sent here to pick up a remedy for one of the sicknesses that had been going around the other children last winter. But she was on an errand, so she did as instructed – said nothing, touched nothing, said nothing but delivered an envelope and waited quietly for the response before running back to the matrons. So, effectively, this was her first real visit to the shop. She did remember the smell, however.

It was a pungent mix of unknown and unknowable ingredients that made both girls sneeze instantly. Their embarrassment was met with a gentle laugh from across the room.

"I can always tell when someone new comes in, the first thing they do is sneeze," the young woman said. She was perhaps as old as the two girls put together, with long red hair drawn back in a handful of small braids, most of which were pulled together behind her head by a soft blue headband. Her green eyes sparkled with laughter when Kari pointed at her.

"You! You were there last night, when - -"

Cousins patted Kari on the shoulder as he edged past her. "Miss Kari, allow me to introduce Briseida, the apprentice who runs this little shop. Lady Briseida, may I present Misses Hikari and Rom – better known to me as Kari and Rom. And the little grey creature with Miss Rom is her companion…?"

"Um, Mully – well, Mulligan," Rom stammered. "But he likes Mully."

Briseida moved past Cousins with a cordial nod of her head, and gracefully gave a slight curtsy to the two girls, and a wink to Mulligan. The randomly assorted beads in her braids clicked and clacked melodiously. Mully lifted his head and sniffed, then lay back on Rom's shoulder, purring with gentle approval.

"Mully thinks you're okay," she smiled.

Briseida looked them both over and cocked an eyebrow. "Well, the first thing we need to do is show you your rooms and get you some new clothes."

Kari looked at Rom for confirmation. "Rooms?" she asked, repeating the word and emphasizing the plurality. "Like, more-than-one-room rooms?"

The older woman smiled and nodded.

"We'd have our own rooms?" Kari asked again.

"Yes, Kari. We have a few spare rooms upstairs, enough for you both to have your own space."

Kari gripped Rom's arm. "This is so strange," she whispered.

Cousins, overhearing her comment, laughed out loud. "You'll love these two, Bree," he said. "They're *so* easy to please."

Kari smacked him in the arm as they passed.

Briseida walked them both out the door at the back of the shop, calling over her shoulder for Cousins to mind the shop for a few moments. He protested, mumbling something about having real work to do, but she ignored him.

She walked the two girls down a gently lit hallway and turned to ascend a carpeted stairway. The darkly stained banisters were finely polished wood and simply carved, and Rom couldn't help but smile as she felt it pass beneath the palm of her hand. Beneath their feet, the boards of the stairs creaked slightly, but were mostly muffled by the carpeting.

At the top of the stairs, they turned the landing and Briseida pointed to two open doors. "These are your rooms, I'll let you two decide which one belongs to which. I chose two with an adjoining door between your closets. Also, at the end of the hall, that last door is the bathroom. You'll still have to share," she explained, "but there are only the four of us, so it shouldn't be so bad."

Rom and Kari nodded, trying to imagine what it would be like to have to share a bathroom with only three other people.

"I had some clothing brought over this morning, I had to guess your sizes, but we can have Sorena – she's a seamstress friend of mine – come back later in the week to do a proper measuring and get you both some dresses that fit you better."

"I like this one," Rom said self-consciously, plucking at the pleats of her dress.

Briseida nodded, and, noticing Kari's expression, added, "Kari, you will have an appointment tomorrow with representatives from the Steamworks guild. They have received a very impressive recommendation from a Professor who knows you, and are sending some people over to talk to you." She took a moment to enjoy the flash of excitement in Kari's eyes before concluding, "Not to be overly optimistic, but I saw fit to add a few pairs of working clothing for you. Dresses may be fitting for a young lady, but are hardly appropriate for the laboratories."

Kari and Rom both restrained squeals of joy before curtseying hurriedly and running into the nearest door. Briseida waited in the hall, silently enjoying the sense of contentment and reassuring feeling that they had made the right choice in bringing the two girls here. The girls were both laughing and debating rapidly as she quietly went back downstairs to make sure Cousins hadn't wandered off; the boy could be trusted with anything of value, certainly, but he could also be trusted to try and avoid anything which smacked of steady employment.

In the end, Rom took the corner room, with one window facing the clock tower across the street, and Kari chose the room closest to the bathroom. The closet which connected their rooms was easily the largest such room either of them had ever seen, and, while not completely filled with clothes, had more fine outfits than they could have dreamed possible. They played an impromptu game of dress up for nearly an hour before finally settling on their clothes.

Rom chose another dress similar to the one she had found in the land of the spirits, but this one was a dark charcoal – nearly black – and she borrowed a pair of boots likely intended for Kari. They were large and black and laced up to nearly her knees, but had good solid soles and weren't too shiny. Kari chose one of the outfits which Briseida had suggested were intended for the laboratory instead of one of the dresses. It had a simple mid-sleeved shirt with a pair of overalls, and a pair of simple brown shoes. The overalls were a bit too baggy, so she tied it off with a thick black belt. The belt had several pouches on it, too, which, though empty, would probably hold a lot of useful things she could find later.

Rom pointed at the belt with an amused expression. "You don't have anything to put there," she laughed.

Kari frowned back at her. "You'll see, I'm going to have lots of things here for all my experiments."

"Yeah, okay, *Professor* Kari."

"You mean 'Steammaster Kari'," Rom's friend teased back, letting the words resound in her ears with a pang of delightful optimism.

The two girls stood and looked at each other for long moments, scarcely recognizing themselves. One day before, they were two different girls, wholly unrecognizable from the two they saw now. Footsteps on the landing interrupted their thoughts. They both turned to see Cousins in the doorway, his eyes were wider than usual.

"Um, Goya wanted to," he cleared his throat, which for some reason was making it harder than normal to speak, "ahem, wanted to see us over in her study."

Mulligan leapt from the bed where he'd been waiting and perched on Rom's shoulder. "Ready," he said.

Rom and Kari both nodded and followed Cousins back downstairs. At the base of the stairs, he took them back up towards the shop, but turned right and into the adjoining building. From here, he led them up a different staircase, one that opened out into a small landing with only two doors. He knocked at the closest door, and "come in" could be heard from within a moment later.

He opened the door and held it for the girls. They entered a room which took up nearly the entire floor and whose windows were all closed off. The room was still relatively well-lit, but all the walls were covered in shelves. Most of the shelves were filled with all manner of books – more than either girl had seen in a single room before – but were also displaying dozens and dozens of curiosities. In the center of the room, beside a metal fixture supporting a glowing yellow perfectly smooth glass sphere, sat an exceptionally old woman. She was dressed in a simple green gown, a colorful scarf draped across her shoulders.

"Welcome to my home, children," she said in a voice whose strength belied her apparent age. "I am Goya. Please close the door behind you and come closer so we can have a little talk."

Chapter 12: The Looking Glasses

Rom paused, one hand on the brass knob. She squinted, trying to be certain of this woman. The old woman smiled, nodding towards her.

"No, my child, I am not the woman who attempted to possess you. I am not *Artifice*."

"But you know about her? I don't know... can you prove that you're not her?"

Goya shook her head. "Our paths have crossed more than once," she admitted. "I am allied with one of her enemies, one whose friends protected you while your soul was far from us. She is far more skilled in the arts of deception than I could hope to challenge – but I can attempt to secure this room with a measure of honesty. But as with all truths, there must at last come a moment where you must *choose* to believe that which you feel is right."

Rom looked at Cousins, Kari and Mulligan, who all nodded quietly. She chewed her bottom lip anxiously, at last deciding that whether the old woman was who she said or not, she couldn't help but feel like more answers would be found here in this room. Rom nodded to Goya, and finally closed the door behind her.

As the door's latch clicked shut, the woman waved one hand in the air – Rom felt the air pressure in the room increase slightly, and Kari stumbled, placing her hands over her ears for a moment.

"What was that?" Kari asked. "It's - - it's gone now, but it was so loud!"

Cousins looked around, confused. "I didn't hear anything. What did it sound like?"

The old woman nodded again. "It was I. I placed a seal upon the room, protecting us from being listened to or spied upon. The spell itself creates no actual sound…except to others who are suitably attuned," she added, looking straight at Kari. "It is as I suspected, child – you have the *gift* within you."

"*What* gift?" Kari asked, taking her hands from her ears.

"I will explain that in a moment," the woman said. "But first, introductions are necessary. There should be no secrets between us."

She pointed towards herself. "I am called Goya. I am a seer, a shaman. I own this small area of land and the buildings upon it, for I have been in this city for most of my life. I am well studied across many of the schools of magic, and am a Master craftsman in several more." She paused long enough for that to sink in, before adding, "I am quite old now – and, before my magical skills begin to fade, am fortunate enough to see the arrival of you three youths, who hold in your hands the necessary abilities to correct the failures of our city – both within and without the Wall."

Cousins looked from her to the two girls and back to Goya. "Um, I don't know--" he began, but she cut him off.

"You are Ballis Furthore, first generation arrival to Oldtown – you were found here when you were scarcely three years old, and you are the last known citizen to have been sent from Aesirium, from Inside the Wall. You have other skills, as well, but I am not at liberty to divulge them at this time; you yourself do not know them as yet. I would suspect you would be disappointed if I revealed them to you before you were ready to know them."

Not giving him a moment to respond, she turned her attention to Kari. "You are Hikari Sandston, only child of Nobumaso and Joriel Sandston. You have a comprehensive love of science; in particular, an unmatched natural understanding for the school of atmology, which I have already taken steps towards granting you full access to. You also possess a natural gift for the perception of magic, which marks you as a candidate for any one of the schools of magic you might be so inclined to study."

"And you," she said, her voice changing in tone as she turned to Rom, "were given the name Rom. You have no given family in the common sense of the word, and as you only too recently discovered, have been marked for great things and powerful responsibilities in this life. Beyond the nature of that purple gem, I have little else I can tell you about your nature that your own disposition has not already confirmed in you, but can assure you that what you perceived was not a dream. You are what they said you are, and what you will do with that only you can say."

Kari turned to Rom, unable to form her question into words.

Rom saved her the effort. "I'm a Reaper," she said.

Cousin's face went white.

The old woman's voice was filled with compassion. "It is true, Cousins. But that calling is not so dreadful a thing in nature as you have often feared. She will present you no harm."

"Why are you telling us this?" Rom asked. She felt angry, but couldn't put her finger on why, exactly.

"Because it is time for you to know," she answered simply. "Cousins, I knew of for many months, now. And he told me before of your apparent sensitivity to magic, Kari." She turned back to Rom. "But you.... I knew of you the moment we found you. Your arrival from the sky marked you as unique, but we could do nothing until you awakened. We were given a very small window of opportunity in which to hide you, mingle you in among the other children and so conceal you from Artifice, who has hungered for you ever since she claimed the life of your predecessor."

Rom's mouth gaped. "Arrival from the *what*?"

Goya sighed, a faint touch of sadness in her voice. "I will explain more to you, later. But I would like first to give the three of you gifts, as proper manners would dictate."

Cousins had looked as if he would have liked to have asked more questions, but the mention of gifts altered his priorities sufficiently to wait. Goya pointed to a small table across the room, which was cleared – unlike the other tables in the room – with the single exception of a pair of strange-looking glasses. They resembled goggles more than anything, with a variety of protrusions and levers surrounding the thick and multicolored lenses.

"Of all the artifacts I have collected over the years, three items here belong to you three children. Those, I call the *Looking Glasses*," she said. "They will show you what you most need. And what you three will most need will be yours." She allowed them a moment for that to sink in, then said, "Kari, dear, why don't you go first? Simply try them on and look around the room."

Rom was glad Goya picked Kari to go first – her own natural suspicion would have kept her from following instructions, but Kari couldn't resist anything remotely technical. Kari slipped them on and turned to face the room, her mouth open in undisguised wonder.

"Wow! Everything's....colorful!" she said. "Everything is glowing and sparkling," she whispered, slowly taking a few steps towards the center of the room. She seemed to lock onto something sitting on one of the bookshelves. Her hands hovered over whatever it was for a few moments, then she looked back towards Goya. "I found it. Now what?"

Goya smiled. "Then you must take them; you are meant to have them."

Kari slid the goggles up onto her forehead and looked more closely, before reaching up and taking them off the shelf – at last, Rom was able to make out what they were. They were a pair of strange gauntlets – metal gloves, far too big for Kari. Kari put one on her right hand – it extended all the way to her elbow before snapping on around the joint of her arm. Although the gloves looked much too large, she seemed to have no difficulty moving the fingers – she was able to put the other gauntlet on her left arm and connect it without challenge.

"These are wonderful! You really mean it – I can have them?"

"They are already yours," Goya nodded, then gestured towards Rom. "Now, it is your turn."

Rom stepped over to Kari, and Kari handed her the goggles, giving Rom a closer look at the gauntlets. They were comprised of hundreds of small plates of metal, beneath which Rom could see the curves of yet hundreds more tiny gears. Each plate had an almost invisible design etched into it – together, these small designs seemed to make some larger pattern on the exterior of the gauntlet, but Rom couldn't make any sense of it. As Rom put the goggles on her own head, Kari had already seemed to lose interest in anything else, focusing herself almost entirely upon the gauntlets themselves.

Taking a slow, deep breath, Rom put on the goggles, and kept her eyes closed for a long moment. At last, she opened her eyes and looked around. Sure enough, as Kari had described it, the room swirled in colors – each object in the room looked like rocks thrown into a pond, sending out perfectly-shaped ripples in all directions that gradually faded into the surface of the water. She looked around the room, taking in each object's color and pattern. Then, two objects jumped out beyond the rest. It was as if they danced there before her eyes or waved their arms to get her attention – obviously they did not, but the effect was the same. She found herself walking closer to them to see more directly what they were.

The larger item was a long pole, taller than she was by at least a foot or more; the top was curved to resemble a crescent moon, and the lower end was curved as well, only more sharply before straightening out to rest on the floor. At the midpoint was a silver-inlaid leather grip, two feet long.

Nearby on the same shelf rested the second item. At first, she thought it was an overly large pendant on an ornate silver chain – but as she moved closer, she saw that it was too large to be worn about the neck. What she had thought to have been the ornament itself was as wide as the length of her thumb, round, with a thick button release at the top at the point where it connected to the chain. She picked it up and depressed the button – the cover snapped open, revealing the face of a watch. The interior of the lid had an unusual design on it which she had never seen before; it looked like a random pattern of overlapping flattened circles with a small dot in a different place on each oval and connected by a series of thinner straight lines. Something about it felt…familiar, somehow, but she couldn't place it.

She looked at the staff but did not touch it. Instead, she held up the watch and turned around to face Goya, who was shaking her head.

"If the glasses show you two things, you should take them both," Goya said. Red faced, Rom turned back and picked up the staff as well before removing the Looking Glasses. She placed the pocket watch in a hidden fold of her dress, clipping the free end of the chain to a small black bow on the opposite side of the dress; Cousins was already standing beside her when she had taken the goggles off.

"So, Goya," he said, "these glasses will show me what I need?"

She smiled. "They show you what you need because I have told you they will do so."

His smile was lopsided. "What do they normally show?"

"They show you the truth of what you ask them to show you."

He nodded, placing them on his head and looking slowly around the room. After a few moments of looking around, he nodded again, and took them off. "Then I already know what gift I need," he said. Holding the goggles up, he grinned. "I choose these."

"They are yours, then, of course," Goya said, nodding.

Cousins smiled and placed the goggles in the breast pocket of his vest.

Goya looked up slowly towards the door. "Ah, I believe Briseida could use some assistance with the preparation of lunch. Would you mind going to assist her?" She waved her hand again, unsealing the room. As the three children said their thank yous and began to leave, Goya motioned to Rom. "Please stay a moment, Rom, could you? I have something else to ask you."

Rom nodded to her friends who left the room, talking cheerfully as they descended the stairs. She felt a strange tingling, like an itching at the base of her neck. Mulligan lifted his head. "My whiskers are twitching, too," he said.

Goya watched the girl for a moment and then turned her head to the side and addressed the open air.

"She knows you are here, Ian, please do show yourself."

A man appeared to one side of them, equally distant from them both. He wore a long blue frock coat with a golden vest and black and white leather shoes. His chestnut brown hair was long, pulled back into a ponytail, and a thin design of hair surrounded his lips and chin. Immediately, however, Rom was struck by the instant sense that he was familiar to her, somehow.

At last, she remembered him from the other day in the market – "You!"

He bowed low to Rom and Goya both. His voice, when he spoke, felt like *springtime*.

"I do humbly make myself known to you, youngest of the Sheharid Is'iin," he said, rising back to his full height. He was thin, but quite tall, with long and expressive fingers; and green eyes that glistened beneath his brown eyebrows. "You may call me Ian," He allowed the statement a long pause before adding, "And I am your brother."

Chapter 13: Of Death, Life & In Between

Rom sat on the floor, resting her head in her hands. "You people need to stop this...for just a moment," she clarified, looking back up at the two concerned adults. "The past two days have been really rough; it feels like someone keeps throwing some new thing at me every five minutes."

Ian nodded. "I am sorry, I was going to wait and tell you later, but..." he looked at Goya accusingly. "You put a truth spell up, didn't you?"

The old woman smiled. "It was leftover from earlier; I hadn't been expecting you."

He sighed. "Well, again, I am most sincerely sorry. See? I can't lie to you about that, even if I wanted to." His playful smile, Goya noticed, was lacking somewhat. It had been some time since they had been together, and for the first time since she had met him, she noticed small creases around his eyes and a few strands of grey in his hair.

Rom looked from Goya to Ian. "So you're one too – a ..." she struggled with the word.

"Sheharid Is'iin? More or less," he replied. He pulled up his left sleeve, which revealed a deep scar on the back of his wrist. "I was awakened as the *Harvester* for this world, more than three hundred years ago."

"Three hundred years?" Rom asked. "You don't look that old."

He smiled. "Benefits of the awakening – it locks us into the time of our transition – or at some relative time thereafter; it is of our choosing. You'll figure that part out when it's time." He had, she was discovering, the annoying habit of walking while he talked; so she was forced to not only follow his words, but follow him with her eyes as he wandered around the room – simultaneously filtering out the various random objects or books he picked up and examined while he spoke.

"Eventually, my partner was moved on to another world and his replacement arrived. She wasn't a newborn, like you are – she was a fully trained harvester like the Is'iin she was sent here to replace. Something about her bothered me – I couldn't quite place my finger on it at the time, but when I had at last discovered her true plans, it was too late.

"What happened to your gem – you had one, right?" Rom asked, pointing to her own gem.

He nodded, pointing to the scar on his wrist. "Artifice stole it from me. To this day, I don't know quite how she managed to do it – but I was able to escape before she could finish me off entirely. Spell for spell, I may have been more powerful than she is, but she was able to surprise me. And now, with my gem in her hands..." He didn't finish the sentence. Rom had seen what she could do, and she could imagine well enough.

"Besides, I never really invested myself into mastering all the powers the spirit gems give us. I know the basics, but I was always more interested in knowledge and magic."

Rom took Mulligan from her shoulder and cradled him in her arms, scratching his head. "What do the gems do? What kind of powers do they give us?"

Ian smiled. "It's easier to show you than to tell you. Why don't I come by tonight and we'll give you your first lesson?" He looked at the staff she had momentarily leaned against a bookcase. "Bring that. And the cat."

Mulligan hissed at him. "I'm not a cat."

Pointedly ignoring Mulligan's refutation, Ian continued, pointing a delicate finger at her feet. "And those are very good boots. *Definitely* wear those. It should be a nice, clear night: good for hunting."

"Hunting?" she asked.

His mouth dropped open, and he turned back to Goya. "You haven't told her?"

"I was going to, before you arrived."

"Tell me what?" Rom demanded. "Don't talk to me like I'm not in the room."

Ian turned back to her, his expression suddenly more somber. "There are always two Sheharid Is'iin on every world; it is a structured and unshakable reality. But one is given to perform the guidance within the world of spirits – that Is'iin spends most of their time in that world, with only a fraction of their time here. The other Is'iin – in this case, you, Rom – spends the majority of their time in this world."

Rom nodded. She could tell Ian was going somewhere with this, but she decided to try and be patient while he got around to it.

"The Is'iin who dwells mostly in their spirit gem is charged with moving souls on to the worlds beyond, particularly the souls who get lost in that world. But the Is'iin who dwells mostly on the world of the physical must bear the charge of moving souls from this world to the next that do not go there of their own accord."

Goya clarified his statement. "You are the Sheharid Is'iin of this physical world, Rom. You will have to find the souls of those who must move on from this world…and force them to move on."

"Force them? How, exactly, do I do that?" Rom asked. Mulligan had crawled back to her shoulder, and she had resumed holding her staff, but her knuckles were turning white; her grip was unconsciously tight enough to evoke a sound like stretching leather.

Ian stepped closer to her, placing one hand on her free shoulder. "We are not saying you must interfere in a person's natural life span – but there are creatures which dwell on past death. They must be found… and destroyed."

Confused by this, Rom asked, "How is that even possible?"

"You are aware," Goya replied, "of the magical shield which protects the city? The one which keeps out all living threats to our citizens during the cover of night?"

Rom nodded. "It hasn't been working so well, lately. The Matrons told us that people were still being attacked at night."

"That is because our Defense guild has not yet discovered a way to bar the way to beings which have died but still dwell upon this world," Goya explained. "And more than ten years have passed since the last Sheharid Is'iin has walked upon the world, and in that time the undead have begun to increase in numbers and boldness."

"Undead?"

Ian shrugged. "It lacks a certain … poetic quality, but it is what they are most often called. Like the Is'iin, there are many names by which they are known. 'Undead' is as good as anything. Their nature, regardless of their species while they lived, is a constant."

"What are they – or, I guess, what *were* they?"

"They were simply wild animals," he explained. "Larger and untamed compared to the ones we have here in Oldtown, but made even worse by…something."

Goya sighed sadly. "Ian and I have been searching for the cause of it, but we have found nothing to explain why the beasts have been driven mad and to the brink of death in such great numbers."

Rom scratched Mulligan behind his ears. "So I would be helping them? Not hurting them?" When they nodded, she added, "And just the…undead animals, right?"

Her eyes on her small friend, she missed a brief exchange of glances between Ian and Goya.

"They are the beings whose souls need to be moved forward," Ian said, choosing his words carefully. Goya's expression was inscrutable, but seemed kind to Rom.

As the young Sheharid considered this, her face evidenced a slow change to her convictions – confusion and dread were replaced by a sense of determination and purpose. "Okay," she said at last, "how do I find them? And how do I kill them?"

"I will show you tonight," Ian answered. "I will return shortly before the sun sets." He bowed low to both Rom and Goya, waved his hand and vanished.

The two stood in silence for several moments, one due to her overwhelming questions and the other out of respect to the young girl's internal conflict. At last, Rom spoke.

"So," she said, simply. Her voice was passionless and even. "I'm a killer."

The old woman shook her head, sadly. "You are what you *choose* to be, child. Your mission is as much one of protector as anything. Few others are capable of physically incapacitating these creatures: between death and life, their strength and physicality is impressive, and they are quicker than the people they prey upon. And they do not completely die easily." She leaned closer, and dropped her voice to a more conspiratorial tone – it had the subconscious effect of causing Rom to listen more intently. "But these creatures – without fail – rarely desire the half-life they live. They seek release – and there is no one else empowered to grant it to them."

Rom looked at her staff. Now that she'd been holding it a while – and now that she had a greater idea of what she was now called upon to do – it didn't really look up to the task. Goya rose from her chair with a prolonged grunt. She shuffled across the floor, past Rom to the shelf by which the staff had been leaning. On the shelf, behind an old pair of soft boots, she picked up a simple silver bracelet.

"You will need this, as well," she said, turning back to Rom and holding it towards her.

Rom looked at it and saw some of the same designs etched into the surface of the staff as on the bracelet, but aside from that and a small black stone, the bracelet seemed unremarkable.

"Put it on," the old woman explained. Rom did so, noting that the bracelet seemed to shrink to more perfectly fit her wrist. It felt cool on her skin. Goya then instructed, "Now press the black gem." Once Rom did, the staff trembled in her hand and vanished. Another push, and it reappeared in her hand.

"You're *kidding*!" she said, a grin crossing her face.

Goya walked closer to Rom, scratching Mully behind the ears before placing her hand on Rom's arm. "It is called the *Shepherd's Crook*. It has many forms, but it is most commonly wielded in that form. It was used by your predecessor, and served him well."

Rom looked towards Goya. "You mean... Ian?"

The old wise woman replied with a nod. "Yes." She motioned towards the door. "But let us speak now of more pleasant things. For example, we need to find you a master under whom to apprentice. Or is there a college in which you wished to study?"

The girl's mind went blank. Although she and Kari had often spoken about that, she'd never really come up with the ideal choice for her. "Um... can I think about it?" She pressed the stone on her bracelet once more, causing the staff to vanish again.

"Of course, of course. In the meantime, I am certain Briseida could use an extra hand in the shop. And when you are ready, I will invite masters here to speak to you until you have found a school in which to train."

They were both quiet as they closed the door behind them and went downstairs to join the others in a light meal. Cousins – in spite of his insistence

that he had many errands that needed tending to –
was still here, eating and laughing beside Kari and
Briseida. On the surface, Rom laughed along with
them, but inside her mind was far away. Mulligan
sat near her on the table, quietly eating his food as
well, and his occasional glances towards her were
deep and comprehending.

Across the street, in the darkened alcove of an
unused doorway, stood a slender man in a dark
jacket and fancy vest. He'd been standing there all
afternoon, but so complete was his affected
demeanor that the few people who wandered past
simply looked through him – within a pair of
steps, they'd already forgotten he was there. It was
a simple enough cantrip, part of the simplest spells
in the guild – sheer first-year material, really, but
one which had infinite uses. It wasn't so much like
an actual illusion, which physically bent the light
and left a tangible warp to those who knew how to
look for it – it simply acted as a passive suggestion
that what was behind the spell just wasn't worth
looking at. The eyes of the passers-by only
remembered the wall, the tree, whatever was
around the caster; and though the mind would've
normally filed their face or appearance away to be
recalled later, now they simply discarded it as
useless data.

He brushed his fashionably unkempt hair back from his face and adjusted his glasses. The lenses had a faintly bluish tint to them – they were charged with a simple spell that allowed him to visibly track a single person wherever they went. They had let him follow his target to this building, and no further – it meant that they had come here and had yet to leave.

Reaching inside his jacket, he drew out a small copper-capped vial of clear liquid. He shook it gently, and, noting no change in color or temperature, replaced it into his jacket. Molla possessed its twin, and if she activated hers, it would trigger a chemical change in both vials. This meant that Molla still wasn't ready for him, so he was content to remain here while he waited for the brat to leave.

The children went upstairs after their meal to talk and muse over their new artifacts, trying to guess just what they might do, although Rom remained very quiet about hers. Once or twice, she pulled out the pocket watch and listened to the mesmerizing rhythm of the gearworks within. Eventually, Cousins looked out one of the windows at the ringing of the bells in the adjacent clock tower and grimaced.

"I've completely thrown away an entire afternoon," he declared. "You should take this as a sign that you're on my good side."

"Good to know," Kari said dryly.

Kari looked over at the silver pocket watch that Rom had tucked into a pocket on her dress for the fourth time in as many minutes. "Why did you pick that?" she asked.

Rom shook her head. "I don't know. It looked pretty, I guess, but...I don't really know why. I didn't really think about it, I just picked it up. What about yours?"

Kari slipped her left hand into one of the metal-scaled gauntlets, flexing her fingers. "It's so wonderful!" she said, grinning broadly as she held her gloved hand close to her ear. "There's leather gloves inside, and it's very soft, but when I move my fingers I can hear all these gears moving around under the metal. These gloves do *something*, I just don't know what, yet."

"Rather makes you wonder why the old woman saw fit to entrust these fantastic items in our young hands, doesn't it?" Cousins ruminated aloud. "She seems to do that a lot - - she generally knows so much more than she says."

Rom rolled her eyes. "At least she doesn't say more than she knows."

Kari laughed, and Cousins merely shrugged. "I just see no harm in opening things to discussion with you," he said. "I get the sense that between the three of us, we are substantially more than our individual parts. Clearly, Goya thinks so as well, but I wish I knew why she felt as such."

"You think too much," Rom said.

He put the glasses on, grinning. "I will leave that to you to decide whether that is a benefit or detriment. For now, I'm off to see where I need to go…" He paused. "That's strange," he said.

"What is?" Rom asked.

"The glasses show me staying here." He turned a dark red at the girl's expressions of horror. "I mean, not HERE, clearly, but here in the shop. Or something. But they definitely show me staying somewhere here, and not leaving."

"They show that?"

Cousins nodded. "It's hard to explain. There are different lenses or filters on these, and each lens lets me see something different, like seeing in the dark, or seeing things close up or far away. One just lets me see…purpose. I've been playing with them, putting coins in hidden places and the glasses always show me where they are, and show me where to walk to find them. They're really quite extraordinary." He took the glasses off, looked around, and then put them on again. Shaking his head, he said, "Still the same. If you will excuse me," he said, moving towards the door, "I need to speak with Goya about this."

Rom and Kari exchanged confusing expressions. He was an odd one, Cousins. Taking the pocket watch out again, Rom listened to the ticking mechanisms behind the ornately- designed face and wondered why it felt so comfortable in her hand.

Chapter 14: Training Begins

Goya confirmed Cousins' suspicions and had him move fresh sheets up to a spare room on the second floor. He spent the remainder of the night taking the glasses on and off, concentrating and putting them back on, walking towards every possible door in the shop and all the windows, growing more and more concerned. Eventually, he gave in and went back upstairs while the two girls helped Briseida prepare dinner.

Halfway through the meal, Rom noticed the darkening skies, and she lost her appetite completely. She pushed the food around on her plate with her fork, and drank most of the juice in her ceramic cup, but her stomach twisted at the thought of more food passing her throat.

Finally, she was distracted by movement in the hall beyond the dining room, and looked up to see Ian standing there, a sword sheathed at his side. Kari saw him a moment later, and jumped up, knocking her chair to the floor – the sudden racket caused Cousins to spin from his chair, while Goya and Briseida held out their hands to try and calm the children.

Kari squinted, pointing at him. "Wait, you're the one who helped carry Rom back – but... you didn't look like...*you*." She blushed and sat back down quickly.

Ian bowed at the waist, arms out from his sides. "My apologies, Lady Hikari – I generally travel with a bit of an artistic element woven about me." He stood straight, and winked to her. "Keeps a popular man like myself from being remembered too carefully."

"It's okay," Rom said. "He's a friend." Mulligan leaped up to her shoulder and she stood up from her chair. "He's going to take me training, I'll be back...ummm?"

"We shall only be gone an hour or so. It is best to not press yourself too hard, too quickly," he explained.

Kari opened her mouth to protest, but Rom waved her off. "I need to learn how to do... whatever it is I do," she said. "He's the only one who can really teach me. I'll be okay."

"Don't worry, Kari," Mulligan echoed. "I'll keep her safe."

"Yeah, I feel a lot better now," she said.

Mulligan made a brief sound of air passing from his lips in obvious annoyance, but Rom moved quickly from the table to avoid any further debate. "I'll be back soon," she said. She double checked to be certain the bracelet was on her wrist – it was on, quite snugly, in fact – and that her pocket watch was secured by its chain. She nodded her head to her friends at the table and turned to follow Ian up the stairs.

At the second floor landing, he walked to the very end of the hall in which was set a darker door, smaller than the rest. Placing one knuckle against the door frame, he whispered a small set of indecipherable words and rapped his knuckle again – and the door opened silently.

"After you," he said, holding the door open for her. Behind the door was another set of stairs, ascending into darkness. "Tell me when you reach the top door – you cannot open that door until this one has closed."

She made her way cautiously, climbing the stairs one at a time until she finally reached another door. "I'm here," she called down, her voice echoing strangely in the darkness. There was a brief moment where the air felt thick and cold, and her ears popped against the increased pressure. A second later, Ian's voice sounded just behind her, causing her heart to pound in surprise.

"Open the door, now, if you please," he said.

She did so, but to an unexpected sight – in front of her was suspended a large trio of bells. Surrounding these were large wheels covered in squarish teeth, fitted together in a dizzying structure. Beyond the bells and gearworks sat the large face of the clock. She instantly recognized the pattern of the numbers as the very clock face across the street from the apothecary. Ian stepped out behind her and closed the door – but when she turned around, no doorway was visible.

"How did you do that?" she asked.

"It's a pretty elaborate structure of spells, really – a portal restructuring spell to connect two unconnected openings – doors, windows, whatever you want; a magical concealment to prevent people from seeing us moving from door to door; and an additional concealing illusion on this doorway into the tower itself so that no one can find their way back into Goya's home."

He seemed very impressed with himself, and Rom was hard pressed to deny him the right. He continued on, "there's also a pair of spells designed to go through the many defensive spells she has on her building, as well as an endurance rune I placed into the wood itself that grounds the entire chain of spells and allows them to continue on without needing me to constantly channel energy into them…" he trailed off, seeing that he had long since lost her.

"Sorry. It's…um, magic."

"Mmm-hmm," she muttered. She was lost in looking out from behind the shutters that framed the clock face, looking across the town. The sun was behind them, and the various rooftops glowed brilliant shades of yellows, oranges and reds, casting a jagged shadow against the tremendous wall. She'd never seen the wall like this, from above the majority of the buildings of her town. It made the wall loom taller than the sky itself, and yet, against the curvature of distance, for the first time in her life she could see both extremes of the wall curve off and around, beyond her sight.

Ian stood beside her. "It rather puts things in a new light, doesn't it?"

She nodded. "I wonder what they're like, inside?"

"Inside the city?"

She nodded again.

Ian chuckled. "Not nearly as exciting as you people are outside the wall," he replied.

Rom turned quickly on him. "You've been inside?"

"I was born there. This out here was a lot smaller, much newer than it looks now. That was back when there were still machines here, working the fields."

She glanced further out the makeshift window, and could see the deepening shadows from the far-distant mountains, but very little of the actual fields. Large lumps of featureless overgrowth cast shadows of their own – some, she knew, were the rusted and useless remains of the cast off machines; others, she had no idea. She tried to imagine the world as it was, but such things were beyond her scope.

Ian waited in silence, let the newly awakened hunter breathe in the city from this first gaze. He knew this moment well; in her own way, she greeted a new perception, even as the old comprehension dwindled into the recesses of her mortal mind. From here, everything below was much smaller than it had been when the sun had risen. Things that had been so insurmountable would now fall away like chaff in the harvest breeze.

He touched her shoulder. "Come. It is time for your first lesson."

They walked to the center of the tower, at the base of a metal ladder that reached up to the rooftop. "Follow me," he said. He placed his hands on the outside rails and kicked off from the floor, sliding upwards to the top support – once there, he rested his feet on the upper rung and slid back the bolt from the roof access, flipping the lid open. He hopped from there onto the roof and out of sight.

Rom stepped onto the ladder, gripping it tightly with both hands. This was higher than she'd ever been, and there was a tightening in her throat as she considered the view she was about to get of the city below. "Hold on tight, Mully," she said nervously.

"Don't worry about me," he said, evoking his most confident voice. "I can fly."

"Hmmm," she replied. She took the rungs one at a time, slowly climbing to the roof. At the top, she stopped counting after 30. She poked her head above the lip of the roof and gasped. The view was even more spectacular here than she had imagined. Holding firmly to the roof, she lifted herself up onto the tiles and stood beside Ian.

"So, Rom," he said, a calmness in his voice which totally contradicted in her mind the fact that they both stood some seventy or eighty feet from the streets below, "what's the furthest you've ever jumped?"

"Um, five meters, I think. Maybe, ten?"

"Hmm," he mused. "And do you know that that is further than most people could possibly jump?"

"I suppose. I'm good at sports and games," she admitted.

He laughed, the sound echoing amusingly from the surrounding buildings. "Well, you're going to jump many times further than that tonight."

"How much further?" she asked.

He looked around them, his eyes settling on a tall building almost as tall as the tower. Its roof was domed, with a narrow spire extending upwards from the center. "See that building over there, with the curved rooftop?"

It was the musical conservatory's Hall of Entrances, she recognized. "Yes, I see it."

"I'm going to show you how to jump from here to there," he said, his voice clearly serious. He was obviously also completely deranged.

"But..." she did the numbers in her head. "It's ten blocks away...that's...." Her math failed her. Kari was the one who did math well. "That's really far."

He laughed again. "By the end of the night, you're going to laugh at how far it seems." He turned to face her. "Let me start by explaining how wrong you are about what you can and cannot do." He reached over and lifted Mulligan from her shoulder. "Here, my little friend, we need to show Rom something important."

She eyed him with a small degree of confusion, mixed with suspicion. He then pointed off directly behind her. "Let's start with that building there."

When she turned around to see which building he indicated, she felt a firm hand in the center of her back, and, next, nothing below her. She looked beneath her to see the street rushing up to meet her. She barely had time to scream.

Strangely, though, she did not. As she approached the ground, things became strange – they began to move in a shimmering blur, shivering, slowing. The wind whipped past her dress, rushed and whistled across her ears and through her white curls. And her feet moved beneath her, meeting the ground with a soft and gentle pause. Her legs bent; her knees took the shock – the dust of the street burst up and away from her in a slowly expanding cloud. Everything stilled – she stopped there a moment, coiled like a spring on one of Professor Theremin's contraptions – and then, in a blindingly swift release, sent her sailing back skywards. The rooftop sped past her – quickly, much too quickly for her to react – and by the time she slowed down, it was further beneath her than the ground was from the roof.

And then – finally – she screamed.

Her feet flailed randomly, her arms waved in a vain effort to gather her balance, and, again, she fell. Speeding past the rooftop, Ian shouted words of advice past the rushing of air.

"Again, but softer!"

As she approached the street, things seemed to slow again – she realized, this time, that it was simply an accelerated perception as opposed to an actual slowing down of the world around her – and she felt her body instinctively react to the approaching ground, coil and absorb the impact. Her legs stored the speed of her descent and waited for her command. She looked up towards the sky, and a hint of a smile creased her lips.

"I can fly," she whispered. And, at least for the space of time between leaps, she did.

After two more attempts, she was better able to gauge the distance from the ground to the top of the tower, and managed an accurate – if not graceful – landing. She was grinning from ear to ear.

"That was wonderful!" she exclaimed. "How far can I jump?"

"On your own, pretty far – like I said, that dome over there won't present much of a challenge to you. But we'll move on beyond that later. For now, you must know that your legs can brace you for as far of a fall as you can jump, and a little beyond; and the further you jump, the faster you are essentially throwing yourself – this means that when you land, you are putting that speed into whatever you land on. If you jump too far, you have to make sure whatever you land on is strong enough to receive you. Do you understand?"

She nodded, although in fact, she was barely listening to him. Her eyes had settled on the curved top of the conservatory, and her teeth were gritted together. Without another word, she kicked off from the roof of the clock tower and sailed across the evening sky towards the Hall of Entrances.

And missed.

She finally came to a bouncing almost-landing two blocks later, rolling to an embarrassing stop against a thick chimney, upside down.

Ian slowly floated down beside her.

"Tsk, tsk," he chided. "Not quite the landing fit for a young lady."

She rolled onto her feet and dusted herself off, too angry at herself to respond.

"Good distance, but terrible aim," he continued. "But we'll work on that later. For now, we have to…" his voice trailed off, for Rom had already jumped again, shrinking rapidly into the distance. Ian shook his head.

"I'm terribly sorry about that," Mulligan apologized. "She's willful."

Ian chuckled. "I was the same way," he confided. "It is how one comes to terms with the new life – we all find our own way, by enveloping ourselves in the sense of what we are in order to erase what we have left behind."

Mulligan nodded. "I think she fell again."

"I can see her," Ian agreed. "We will follow her, though not too closely."

He looked towards the fields and saw a brief spark of blue flash across the defense shield. "She is already following her instinct," he observed, seeing Rom's next jump take her in that same direction. "Come, little friend, she is about to have her first true test."

Mulligan said nothing, simply held on tightly as Ian cast another simple spell to send them reappearing at the point where Rom would most likely intercept the invading creature.

Chapter 15: Drawing the Crook

Rom pulled herself back up onto the roof of the granary, grumbling to herself about the slippery qualities of dust. She was already much improved at the jumping and the landing, but was still struggling with the proper gauging of distances. She sat down on the eaves of the rooftop, letting her feet dangle in a manner she would have thought dangerously precarious only an hour before. The stars were incredible tonight – not only the small points of flickering lights, but the broad band of smaller, more dimly shimmering bits were visible. And yet... amid the sense of peace she thought she might otherwise feel, there was an increasing shiver of anxiety disrupting her tranquility. Something was not right.

Her breathing, her pulse – everything became silent at once, so much so that she was aware of Ian and Mully's arrival before they could speak.

"There's something here," she whispered.

Mully landed on her shoulder. "It's one of the monsters you have to fight," he replied softly into her ear. It tickled her, but she did not flinch.

Stepping to the other side of her, Ian crouched low. "One of the gifts of the Hunter is the ability to sense when creatures are near whose souls have not continued on. They feel that the world is out of balance, and you can use that natural ability to track your prey."

She pointed to the far intersection, which was unlit by the irregular street lamps. "It's there, hiding in the shadows," she said. Ian nodded.

"Draw the Crook," he said.

She tapped the black stone on the back of her bracelet, and felt a surprising relief as the cold weight of the shepherd's staff fell into her hand. It shivered in her hand, like a thing alive.

"The staff knows what it must do, as well – you only need to allow it to work," he said.

It was unnerving to her at first, because just as he said, the staff continued to pull at her, as if it were anxious to fight. But looking down into that blackened pit of shadows made beads of sweat appear on her forehead. Her spirit gem was glowing, but not producing nearly enough light for her to see – she would have to drop down and confront a creature which could likely see her much more easily than she could see it.

"How can I fight something I can't see?" she asked.

She could hear the sympathetic smile in Ian's voice. "The staff knows what it must do," he repeated.

She nodded, not quite understanding but prepared to accept it. "Hold on, Mully. We're going."

His claws dug into the fabric, giving her a brief moment of discomfort to help her ignore the fear that welled up in her heart. With staff in hand and her small friend on her shoulder, she took a deep breath and leapt off into the shadows.

The second she landed, the staff pulled sharply to the left in a grand arc. It was nearly humming as it cut through the night air, and she had the momentary sensation that she was swinging through the branches of a bush – dozens of small impacts skittered off the ends of the staff, accompanied by a loud, low hissing sound from somewhere just over her head.

For a moment, the staff started to pull her forward, off balance, and she struggled against it. But then something heavy struck against the back of her head, sending her rolling across the cobblestones of the street and scrambling for footing. She nearly tripped over the staff when it next pulled sharply to the right, but this time she moved with it, and felt relief when a fast burst of wind whipped past her arm. The staff did know what to do – so she stopped fighting against it and allowed it to guide her.

It urged itself upwards and horizontal, blocking a pair of attempted strikes, and then spun in a vicious circle over and down. Bright blue sparks erupted across the area as the top curve of the staff struck the hardened carapace of a huge insect. Rom was glad now that she hadn't seen it from the rooftop – she might not have jumped down if she'd had a decent look at its long, snakelike body and countless hairy legs. She'd seen this sort of thing in the field, but they were usually only a few inches long – this one was probably ten times as long as she was tall. A few words the Matrons would never have forgiven her for saying escaped her mouth, but she focused on the task at hand.

The staff was getting easier to wield, she noticed – at first, it seemed like it was making very strong movements, almost like it was trying to teach her. Now, it was very subtle: a slight twist here, a gentle leaning there, and she could sense what it wanted her to do beyond just swinging and blocking. She landed another two or three strikes on the beast, each one creating a shower of blue light in the plaza.

Mully spoke to her, his voice calm and insistent. "Its shell is too strong for the staff," he said. "You'll have to strike it on its belly – or in its face." It made sense; it didn't even seem to notice her previous contacts.

The trouble with trying to hit this thing where he'd suggested was that all of its legs and teeth were there – so positioning herself for an attack on its relatively unshielded underside meant putting herself directly in line with its ability to strike back. But just then, the staff pulled up and back – hard.

She kicked up and over, just as a flash of something heavy struck the ground just where she'd been standing – whatever it was, it had hit the ground hard enough to split stone. When it pulled free, it sounded like steel drawn across a whetstone.

"What was *that*?" she nearly yelled.

"It was his tail, I think," Mully answered. "It has a big pointed end on it, about half as tall as you are."

Rom sighed. This wasn't getting any easier. What good was a staff going to be against something like that? She needed some sort of shield – or a weapon that could work as a shield AND a weapon.

The staff began to move in her hands, so suddenly that she nearly dropped it. Its center of gravity was changing, the handle became shorter. She almost laughed out loud when she realized she was holding… a parasol.

A blur of motion in the deeper darkness moved towards her, a flash of shadow – the parasol snapped open, and, to Rom's amazement, actually blocked the tail-spike. Although she could feel a degree of the impact in the handle, it deflected the stinger itself, sending it crashing back to the street.

"Oooh," she laughed softly. "Magic parasol."

She spun the parasol over in her hand as it closed up and brought it crashing down on the tail while it attempted to dislodge itself, snapping the spike cleanly from the giant insect. Its hiss changed to a high-pitched scream, and, with a hundred heavy thuds of its feet, began to move quickly away from her.

It was running now towards a well-lit corner – it seemed to prefer the dark, but in its pain and panic, it was probably just finding the quickest path to the open fields. She jumped hard and fast to try and arrive at the opposite corner and trap it in the light. As she sped over and past it, she could feel the parasol shifting back to the shepherd's crook. The staff knew the fight was coming to a close.

Managing to turn in the air, she landed with a slight skidding on the stone streets, once again facing the creature. Now in the light, it was even larger than she'd thought – before, it was mostly curled in upon itself – protecting its clearly vulnerable underside – but now it was moving in a straight line, all its legs pumping madly, desperate for the safety of the underbrush outside the city streets.

She raised the staff over her head, twirling it in a fierce spin which generated a low howling noise like the mad winter winds past the eaves. It was enough to cause the millipede to pause in concern. With a quick hop-step, she closed the distance between them and brought the staff down hard against the side of its head, making it draw up in reflexive defense of its feelers – as soon as it did so, the staff spun completely around again in her hand, and, with both hands firmly on the handle, struck it squarely on the underside of its head, just below the snapping mandibles with a physically audible crack.

The blue sparks again erupted, but this time began to spread across the surface of the creature. All its arms and appendages began to twitch violently, and it screamed again.

"I think we better stand back," Mulligan suggested, and Rom agreed, taking another hop backwards from the monster. It was convulsing now, its tail whipping about and still oozing from the wound she had previously given it.

She was only distantly aware that Ian was now standing beside her. "It fights against death," he said. "Something – some reason, or something more – bonds it to this world. You must sever that."

Rom was about to ask how she might accomplish that, when she felt the staff shift one final time. The handle twisted, became longer, and the top felt heavier. She knew the long, curved blade was affixed to the top of the staff even before she looked at it. They'd talked about this tool in the agriculture classes in the orphanage – it was called a scythe. It was used for harvesting. She nodded silently. She knew what to do, but in spite of this knowledge, a coldness crept up beneath her skin. The scythe felt different than the other forms her Crook possessed; there was a permeable sentience to it – it felt *alive*.

She stood in renewed silence, waiting for the creature's movements to slow. At last, it simply shuddered on the stones of the street.

"Careful," Mully urged.

Nodding, she stepped closer, towards the shivering head of the long millipede. As she raised the blade back in a fearful arc behind her, the creature paused, tilting its head towards her. In the sodium yellow lights of the street, she could see herself reflected from the many onyx beads of its eyes. There she was, an eleven year old girl in a charcoal dress and a pet flying (and speaking) cat. A fearsome yet empathetic figure of death itself: a harvester, a reaper. A Sheharid Is'iin. A merciful agent of the world of the spirits.

In her heart, she heard the creature concede: it was time to die. The air whistled past the blade as it passed through the head of the beast without a visible trace. One more twitch, and that was all. It was gone, leaving only its body behind. In her mind, she heard its gratitude.

The scythe remained for a long moment as if breathing the air, before shifting back to the original form of the shepherd's crook. She stared at it for the space of several breaths, at last dismissing it with a gentle press of the bracelet's stone.

Ian stepped from the shadows to stand beside her, and led her back to a nearby rooftop.

"Ian?" she asked. "Was this what it was like for you?"

"Yes," he whispered.

She was silent for another while, but then said, "The others I met – Memory, Force and Inertia – they could all do things based on their names. Or their names were based on what they could do, they never really explained that."

Ian smiled kindly. "It is a little of both, in fact," he said.

She turned to face him. "What about you? 'Ian' isn't really a Sheharid name, then, is it?"

He breathed out slowly through his nose. "It is the name I took when my gem was stripped from me. Before then, I was known as Passion."

Rom's face wrinkled. "Passion? Sounds like a pretty dumb power."

He laughed. "It did have its uses. But mostly, it was very helpful in understanding people, or helping to control people's fears or anger."

"Is it all gone, then?" Rom asked. "All the powers you had as a Sheharid?"

Nodding slowly, he answered. "The power went with the gem."

She paused a moment, then quickly stepped closer and hugged him, briefly. "I'm sorry," she said.

He patted her hair. "Do not be," he said. "Had it not happened this way, I might never have had the pleasure of meeting you."

She let go, stepping back and biting the inside of her cheek to keep herself from letting her emotions escape her. It wasn't enough, all the responsibility she was beginning to feel, to then add a large share of guilt for events she'd had no power to stop.

To Ian, she said simply, "Are we done learning?"

"For tonight," he replied.

That was a good enough answer for her. She looked back at him, noted the somber expression on his face, and nodded. With a slight movement of her foot, she leapt the thirty-plus feet to the next rooftop and began the short journey back to the apothecary.

Chapter 16: Never Use a Strange Pistol

Kari couldn't fall asleep. She'd reluctantly gone upstairs with Goya's reassurances that Rom would be in good hands with that tall stranger, but she felt uneasy about him. She recognized him from the other night when he'd helped Briseida tend to Rom's injuries and carried her all the way back to the Orphanage, but it was strange that she hadn't *remembered* that she remembered until just then at dinner. Something about him was vibrantly magical, she could barely hear anything but the music when he was around. She had asked Goya about the music she could hear after Rom and Ian had left.

"Where is that music coming from?" she'd asked.

Briseida and Goya exchanged knowing looks. Goya explained, "What you are hearing, Kari, is not actual music. It is the language of magic, spoken only to those who are either extensively trained in hearing it, or those rare few who have the natural ear to perceive it."

Kari looked over at Cousins. "That box you had – something inside it was singing like that, too," she said. All eyes at the table focused on the young man – an experience of which he was less than fond.

Cousins sighed, running a nervous hand through his light straw-colored hair. "Okay, yes. I probably shouldn't have involved you girls. But there were unfortunate circumstances."

Briseida spoke up in his defense. "Kari, it was a favor I asked of him. What he carried had significant value, and we needed to be certain it was not acquired by undesirable parties."

"What was it?"

Briseida stood and walked into the other room. A few moments later, Kari could hear the sound again – faintly, but growing in volume. When Briseida returned, she was carrying the small box. She opened it and placed a small leather pouch on the table in front of Kari.

"Go ahead – you may open it."

Kari loosed the drawstring and emptied the contents carefully into her hand – a single rock, smaller than the palm of her hand. It was a deep yellow in color, nearly opaque, with a series of random lines crossing the interior that made it appear cracked and broken. For a moment, it simply looked like a smoothly polished, egg-shaped stone. But after resting in her palm, it began to glow brightly, the volume increasing dramatically as well. She winced, startled, and dropped the stone onto the table. There, the glowing dimmed and the music resumed its previous tone.

Cousins was staring. "Okay, that, even *I* heard for a moment," he said, breathless with wonder.

Goya nodded. "You have indeed a rare gift, child. Rarely does a Morrow Stone react so strongly with someone untrained."

Kari stared back down at the rock. It didn't look significant, really. Smooth and shiny, perhaps, but it didn't seem particularly wondrous. "A *what* stone?"

"A *Morrow Stone* is a rare object – a storage fount of art," Briseida explained. "Legends used to speak of these as being items of unimaginable power – magicians of old were said to use them to store their artistry, their energies. It has been suggested that some have even pressed their very souls into them, giving other magicians the opportunity to draw on that magical essence."

Goya took a drink from her glass and set it back down. "They were patterned after the spirit gems of the Sheharid Is'iin," she said. "But where those gems were a natural extension of their arts, the Morrow stones were a constructed fusion of magical energies into stone. But the process of their construction has been lost to time – no new Morrow stones have been made in more than a hundred years."

Kari continued to examine the stone, turning it over slowly in her hands, staring intently at every line, texture and color within the stone. It was certainly different than anything else she'd ever seen – and the pattern of the music she could distinctly hear emanating somehow from within it started to make sense to her. She realized she knew the notes enough that she found herself starting to hum along with it, but at that point, Briseida held her hand out for the stone. Reluctantly, Kari gave it back to her and felt a strange sadness as the music faded while Briseida put the stone away.

The topic changed to other things – some of the day to day happenings in the shop, and so forth, when Kari caught herself yawning. Goya herself mentioned being rather tired, and they all made their way off to their rooms for the night. Briseida was the last to go upstairs, first making the rounds to the doors and windows and securing the building for the evening.

The song wouldn't leave Kari's mind, however. She lay in bed and could hear it playing, over and over. When she had first heard the music, it had seemed more like a series of wordless tones, but the more she listened to it in her mind, she noticed that there were actually words and structure to it. Embedded in the pattern of the notes, there were distinct verbal tones and sounds – she couldn't figure out what kind of language it was, but she couldn't help thinking that she could come to understand it if she could simply break it down enough.

Her thoughts fluttered, wavered - - something distracted the threads of the music's puzzle that was attempting to unravel in her mind. It was soft, but close – her eyes snapped open when it occurred to her that it was another series of notes. Someone else was using some sort of magic nearby! Her first thought was that it was likely Goya or Briseida, but something about the tone in the music felt unusual, somehow different than what she would expect either of the women to use. There was an accent to it, a different voice generating the notes. Also, the music felt hushed, like someone was trying to sing and not be heard.

Uncertain of exactly why she was worried, she got out of bed quietly and crept to her door. She listened there, but heard nothing but the faint strains of the same music. This music, she could now tell, was very distinct from the Morrow Stone's melodies – in fact, she could almost immediately pick apart the pattern and structure of this. There was an almost masculine energy about this; it was most certainly not either of the two older women who lived here. And it wasn't Cousins – she generally felt no sense of art about him at all, it couldn't be anything he was creating. Her eyes widened. *An intruder*!

She listened again at the door, trying to see if she could understand where it was coming from – it seemed relatively close, but then again, not too near - - deciding it was probably downstairs, she slowly opened the door to her room, careful not to allow the door catch to snap open or closed as she did so.

She and Rom had learned long ago how to walk on wooden floors without letting them creak; she kept to the wall, where the support was more stable and less likely to allow for temperature or moisture expansion of the planks. Slowly, she made her way down the hall towards Cousin's room, even as she continued to listen to the magical tones and tried to understand its nature. It was a spell of some sort, she could tell; but what was its purpose? What was the magic effect being attempted? What were they doing? Who were they?

Nearly halfway to Cousin's door, she realized that the pattern of the art was too structured, too flawlessly stable to be done by a person – it had to be some sort of active device. She wasn't sure why she knew that, but it made sense, somehow. She frowned. What if that device could be activated and allowed to repeat its spell without the caster being nearby? Not a good thought, she realized. If that was the case, the intruder could be anywhere. They could even be up here on the same floor as she was.

A momentary rise of panic flooded through her, breaking her concentration – the sound of the magic faded, replaced by a far too loud creak of a board beneath her foot. She froze in her steps, too late.

Movement appeared from the shadows ahead of her, between her and Cousin's door. A woman turned to face her, a white mask pulled snugly across her face to just above her lips. From neck to toe, she was dressed in a black suit, buckled down one side. Across her shoulder was slung a small pack, with a holster strapped to her opposite hip and tied across at the middle of her leg. Both hands were gloved, with the fingertips exposed. Above the mask were a pair of goggles, and a long ponytail was visible behind her left ear.

The woman raised one index finger to her lips and pointed back towards Kari's room with the other. But if she thought Kari too afraid to respond, she was mistaken.

"HELP!" Kari screamed.

"Damn it," the woman hissed. The gun at her side was immediately in her hand – she spat out one word: "Sleep!" as she pulled the trigger.

Cousins threw open the door just in time to see Kari collapse, a strange woman pointing a gun towards her. Without a second thought, he charged her from behind, driving his shoulder into her arm and sending the gun flying from her hand. They both collapsed onto the floor but Cousins was the first back onto his feet, scrambling for the gun. He'd seen this gun before, they called it a "Spellshot" – instead of the iron or wooden balls most such pressure-employed firearms employed, this one had a cartridge of single-use magical shells, which were either permanently charged or relied on a short-term command from their wielder.

Life on the streets had taught him to work the odds. Picking up the gun, he drew it aligned on the masked woman and called out "stun!" as he pulled the trigger. A red flare of light burst from the barrel, knocking him backwards towards the wall. He gritted his teeth in fury as an invisible force paralyzed him and caused him to drop to the floor.

The woman's lips curled in a grin. "Silly boy," she purred. "Don't you know never to pick up a stranger's gun?"

She bent over and pried the pistol out of his sluggish hand. "Mine's got a devastating safety feature," she whispered. "Just be glad you weren't shooting to kill."

She holstered the gun and looked him over. "You don't have it on you, do you? Hmmm. But Favo says you had it when you got here, so you must have given it to *them*." She frowned, taking a cursory look back around the second floor landing.

"Not even any shields up here, so it must be back downstairs." She looked back to Cousins. "Don't go anywhere," she said. "We'll be back to talk to you if we can't find it."

Chapter 17: Favo Carr

Favo. There was no need to specify a last name to him; there was only one man named Favo of any note in the town; Favo Carr. Cousins was a well known name on the streets, but among most circles he was just considered "a kid who knows a guy", the sort of young person people sought out for the random errand; for the casual introduction. He had a reputation for following through, keeping trust, and honesty. At the least, he never gave away anyone's secrets, and, in his line of work, confidentiality had a serious amount of value.

Favo Carr had a different reputation. He was a bit more than ten years Cousins' senior, and had made a strong name for himself early on in his career as a petty thief. He was arrested by the Defense Guild, but being only 14 years of age, had his sentence commuted in exchange for an apprenticeship by a professor of the school of Kinesthesiology; the judges supposed that a year or two under the tutelage of an institute of science might give Favo the discipline he obviously lacked. What they did not know was that Favo's new guardian, Mason Boggard, had a series of debts owed to certain unsavory elements of their city, and needed a means of acquiring money and goods in a way the college and his peers could not discern.

Boggard taught Favo not necessarily the standard courses in magic, but rather taught him an applied series of lessons and loaned him a variety of artifacts which allowed Favo to bring in a substantial quantity of wealth. However, Boggard was not satisfied with simply paying his debts – he continued to utilize Favo to make him substantially well off, meanwhile affording the young man an education in crime and subterfuge.

What Boggard did not foresee was that his own greed would imprint itself on Favo, as well – and eventually Boggard's crimes were anonymously revealed to his collegiate board of magistrates, who divested him of his position and title, delivering his substantial assets to his only heir – his ward, Favo. A few years later, Boggard himself was found dead in an alleyway, a casualty of his own unpaid debts to others of Oldtown's dark underworld.

Favo, having made many contacts across the town itself, left the college but thrived as an independent entrepreneur – he opened a series of private investment houses, which were in fact little more than a front for his operations. People who were privy to such things knew that if there was something that had to be done, acquired, or removed, no matter the cost, Favo could get it done. Even the defense guild had sought his services on occasion – there were things even they were uncomfortable doing. Favo, as such, became at the young age of a mere 25, one of the most notorious and acceptably ruthless names of Oldtown-Against-the-Wall.

Cousins had been trying to avoid Favo ever since he'd been tasked with delivering the box to Goya. Favo and his second-in-command, Molla, had almost caught up with him a week ago, when Cousins had had the good fortune to cross paths with Kari and Rom. He'd left the box with them long enough to be able to convince Favo he didn't have it as well as sincerely convince him that he didn't know where it was. It wasn't that Cousins had a problem with lying, it was just that he knew Favo well enough to know he tended to use magic in his work. The simplest way to beat a *Veracity* spell was to tell the truth – the key was to arrange the facts so that you could *literally* tell the truth, but conceal what you did not want to be caught with.

Evidently, Favo had decided to keep tabs on Cousins anyway. He wanted to kick himself – he should've understood the Looking Glasses' meaning when they told him to stay. Clearly, Favo must have been waiting for him to leave.

He wasn't sure how long the paralysis would last, but judging by Molla's reaction, he was probably going to be like this for a while. Thankfully, he was frozen in such a way that he could both see – and be seen – as the door swung open at the far end of the landing. Rom and Ian stepped from the doorway, turned and instantly saw Cousins and Kari laid out on the floor.

Ian held up a hand for caution, and they both stood stock-still to analyze the situation. The man placed a calming hand on Rom's shoulder – it was clear she wanted to instantly run to Kari's side – and nodded, silently assuring her that her friend was well. He reached into his jacket and drew out a thin piece of paper, no larger than the palm of his hand – there was some sort of design on one side, like a playing card. He waved it once in the air and then flicked the card quickly from him. It sailed for five or six feet and then stopped, as if striking an invisible *something* before fading into a small breath of smoke. He then turned to Rom and nodded. To Cousins, he said, "They cannot now hear us. We have a few moments to prepare."

They walked quickly to Kari, and Ian held his hand above her, palm towards the ground. "She is only asleep. You may wake her, but gently," he cautioned. While Rom knelt beside her and nudged her softly by the shoulder, Ian moved on to Cousins.

He pulled out another piece of paper from his inner pocket and placed it against Cousin's forehead. From this side of the paper, Cousins could see the images, but his eyes – held as they were by the spell – could not focus clearly enough to see what they were. There was a faint spark and the card dissolved, sending warmth across his skin, which was followed by a dull ache in his bones and muscles – however, the paralysis vanished.

He stood unsteadily, teeth gritted. "Please tell me we're going to stop them," he growled.

Ian nodded. "Fetch your glasses."

Downstairs, Favo checked the color on the amulet. It was growing dark; they probably only had another five or ten minutes before they'd be setting off whatever alarms the old woman had on this place. He'd gone through the logical spots in the shop's back office, but he still couldn't find it. *It's the problem with stealing from magicians*, he thought, *they always have the best hiding places.* He ran a hand across his unshaven jaw. This was taking too long.

Molla appeared in the doorway. "It was a girl," she said. "I put her to sleep."

He arched an eyebrow.

"*Just* to sleep," she said. "I didn't hurt her."

He nodded, satisfied. He didn't care what his reputation was; a person never had to look their reputation in the face before they slept at night. He had struggled for years with the delicate balancing act required to keep his business affairs clean, free from the sort of thing that a simple apology or a bag of economical reparations couldn't resolve. Molla was a good person to have around during a job, but she had always been possessed of a substantially distinct set of priorities.

"I heard a boy's voice," he commented, pulling two additional drawers out and looking quickly through them.

Molla chuckled low in her throat. "The Cousins brat again. He tried to get a shot off; I left him stunned in the hallway."

Favo grimaced. Cousins was starting to become a problem. As it was, the boy's influence in the town was growing substantially, but the biggest concern was that Favo actually liked the boy; made Favo think of himself, had he made different choices.

"Still nothing," Molla said more than asked. Favo shook his head no, and kept looking in the cabinets.

Molla slammed one of the drawers closed with an exasperated sigh. "I still say we bring the shop girl or the two brats down here and encourage one of them to tell us."

"I told you, she's probably more than just a simple shop girl," he said. "She's the old woman's apprentice, after all." Molla's impatience was rubbing off on him, and he pointed a thumb towards the opposite wall. "And the children are options, but not yet. You want to be helpful, go check that side of the room."

Before she had a chance to argue, he added, "Three minutes, we're out. Make them count."

She adjusted the mask across her face and nodded. She couldn't really argue with him, he was always right about these jobs. At any rate, she'd be glad to wrap this up and get home. This mask was hot and making her sweat.

When she moved past Favo, a slight breeze followed her and brushed against him. He smiled at the scent. It reminded him of the purple blossoms that arrived each summer after the late spring rains. That made him think of his youth in the fields, tending to the crops and helping them get every last drop of water they needed. The summers were hot. Days of standing beneath the sun, its rays pounding down on them like... he shook his head.

He was standing in front of the first row again – but hadn't he already checked that row? And why was he thinking about his childhood? Work to be done, no time for daydreaming. It was a good childhood, he mused, full of daydreams. Warm, lazy days in the grass, cool evening breezes blowing the… he shook his head again. *Damn it*. What was happening? He was back at the first row again. What was he looking for, he wondered? Why was he - - -

He gritted his teeth and slapped the back of his glove. "*Purgios*!" he called out.

He grabbed Molla by the arm, where she was flicking her hands in the air as if chasing fireflies. She snapped back to attention. "What? What's going on?" she demanded.

Pointing to the doorway, he turned her to face it. "Give us a wall, I need a second."

She looked up to see a façade splintering in the air to reveal a tall, thin man and two children. But Molla was no novice. She quickly threw down a pebble from a concealed pocket into the doorway, which sprang up into a thick rock wall that blocked the two of them in and kept the others out. "Done!" she called to Favo.

He looked at her shoulder and brushed away a small spot of dust. "They hit you with a muddler, you must have dragged it in here with me. We have to go – our time is up." He was pulling out a small pouch from his belt, and emptying a handful of sand into his palm. Only enough for one of these cabinets, he measured, frowning. He flipped a coin in his mind and decided on the opposite result, just to counter the potentially bad luck of instinct. Blowing the sand onto the cabinet, he took three steps backwards and ran into the cabinet at full speed. The cabinet vanished with a loud popping sound, knocking him backwards across the room.

"If it's still in this room somewhere, then they deserve to keep it," he said.

She shrugged, pulling a small metal tube from another pocket. "We'd better go, or they might deserve to keep us, too."

He looked around the four walls, the ceiling, the floor. They were out of time, and out of options. He pointed to the floor. "Fancy a swim?"

Her frown, visible below the mask, was filled with disgust. "You're going to have to clean me off when we're done with this," she said.

He chuckled as she unwound the wax seal on one end of the tube and pointed the compressed steam cannon towards a spot on the floor, halfway between them both. "Perhaps we should start escaping from all our little adventures through the sewers," he grinned.

She pulled the protective goggles over the eye holes in the mask. "Don't push it," she growled, holding her breath.

"Was that the woman that knocked you out?" Ian asked Cousins, after the stone wall sprung up in front of them.

Cousins nodded. "I think it's Molla," he explained. "She's one of the only women he works with. Hard to tell with that mask, but I'm pretty sure it's her, by the voice."

"Very well," Ian answered. "Rom, I'm going to need you to kick this stone wall in," he said. "Do you think you can do that for me?"

Rom looked at him like he had just asked her if she were made of cheese. "You tell me – all I know is that I can jump far and kill monsters."

"*Kill monsters*?" Cousins asked.

"Later," Ian interrupted. "Rom, quickly – it's just like jumping, only you're going to have to jump two directions at once – towards the rock and immediately against it; and you have to jump harder than you've ever jumped. You can do this."

She nodded, taking the queue from the intensity in his explanation. Figuring her right foot was the stronger of the two, she took a step backwards and kicked off with that foot, slamming both feet at once into the center of the stone. Rather than bracing herself like she did when landing on the street, she kicked out fiercely. Surprisingly, the entire wall imploded into a puff of smoke, seemingly compressing into a tiny pebble. Without the rock as an opposing object, Rom flew on ahead and through the doorway, crashing into a stack of boxes on the far side of the office.

Ian and Cousins looked into the room, but quickly realized that Rom was the only other occupant – and a gaping hole in the center of the room made it clear where the two thieves had gone.

At that moment, Briseida and Kari appeared behind them. Ian quickly brought them up to speed.

Rom pointed down at the hole in the floor. "Should we go after them?" she asked, holding her nose.

Ian shook his head. "They will likely leave a path of traps behind them; by the time we made our careful way through them, they would be long since vanished."

Cousins agreed. "He's got a lot of skill, that one. Not the kind of fellow I'd want to tangle with down in a dark tunnel."

Briseida examined the hole. Whatever they had used to get through the stone, it had burst a solid hole through ten inches of reinforced stone, plus an inch thick of iron plating.

"I've never seen arts like this," she commented, "It was strong enough to carve this hole through the entire floor and burst out the underside."

Ian frowned. "I cannot sense the echoes of the magic they used." Turning to Cousins, he asked, "You are familiar with this man, Favo, yes? What forms of magic does he use?"

Cousins shrugged. "Magic isn't truly my strong hand," he admitted. "That's the details what interest you and your sort," he winked at Kari. "I do know he does a good deal of under-the-table business with the crafting guilds, so I'd wager his talents are manufactured, rather than learned."

Kari was looking down at the hole and missed the gesture. Running her fingers along the lip of the opening, she lifted them to her nose. "That's condensation," she said. "And it's pretty warm. I don't think they used magic; I think they used some kind of compressed steam."

Skeptical, Cousins asked, "Are you sure? I've never seen some damage like that caused by air."

"Steam isn't just air," she chided. "It's very hot water – and, directed appropriately, it can move with great speed."

"She would know," Rom teased. "She knows *everything* about that."

Kari blushed. "Well, not *everything*: I don't know how they got steam to do *that*. But I'm pretty sure they used steam here, somehow." She looked more closely into the opening, and scrunched up her nose. "Eew. Stinky. Oh, and I think they cracked one of the distribution pipes down there, I can hear it hissing." Sitting back up, she looked at Briseida and Ian. "We're going to have to patch that up or it could burst. And that would be *bad*."

Ian slid off his jacket and knelt beside Kari by the hole. "Show me what needs to be done, and I will do what I can."

A few minutes later, following Kari's beaming assurance that the pipes were "shiny like new," Briseida pulled a small rock from one of the remaining shelves' many drawers. Scraping it first on the edge of the floor, she dropped it into the opening. It hung there, as if suspended on an invisible thread, and then expanded rapidly to fill the gap. "I will speak with one of the engineers tomorrow and ask them to flush out any remaining traps left by the thieves and to put a more permanent seal on our foundation. But for now, it is time to return to bed," she said conclusively. She looked at Ian and said nothing more, but he nodded.

The children were led back upstairs in spite of their protests and eventually managed to fall asleep, as the rush of adrenaline gradually left their systems.

On the other side of the building, Briseida and Ian met briefly with Goya to review the night's excitement.

"Did they find the stone?" she asked them.

Briseida shook her head. "They did manage to take a good deal of herbs and minor talens," she said, "but they were looking in the *office*."

Goya smiled. "You were right to conceal it as you did, apprentice. Perhaps an old woman like myself is far too linear to think as cleverly as you younger witches do."

Ian arched an eyebrow. "Does the girl even know she carries it?"

The young woman shook her head slightly. "She and Cousins both believe they saw me take the stone back and put it away in another room. It will be safer for now, where it is."

"Clever, indeed," Ian said, clearly impressed. "A minor suggestion, but a simple enough one to be overlooked by the thieves if they had thought to discern it through the children's minds."

"Precisely."

Goya's smile faded: back to the business at hand. "Ian, would you mind locating this Favo lad for us? He is employing a variety of magical items, including the gem he used to attempt to pass my wards, which are of a both rare and inestimably old craft. I would be surprised to find he had constructed them on his own."

"You suspect he is working with someone else?"

"He has an entire organization, but I've only seen him operate in the field with his assistant, this Molla woman." She looked meaningfully towards Briseida as she said this.

Her apprentice lowered her head in a slow and remorseful nod. "So you believe it is her, after all? That she is not dead?" Briseida wrung her hands anxiously, twisting an elegant ring she wore on one hand.

"I believe she has a strong will, and it would take more than death or exile to be rid of her. We are fortunate she did not see you, or this evening might have gone in another direction." To Ian,

245

Goya continued. "His associates are not our greatest concern, my old friend. There is only one person for whom he could be employed, only one who would pay him for the object he seeks."

"You suspect…?" He did not need to finish the sentence, he and the old woman both knew of whom they spoke.

Briseida considered a moment, and sighed, echoing their thoughts. "Artifice."

Goya looked again at Ian.

"The signs continue," he said sadly.

She nodded, adding, "As does my hope."

Chapter 18: Always in Motion

In the morning, Cousins and Ian had already left, leaving Rom and Kari alone to help Briseida with breakfast and the morning chores. Rom and Kari had spoken until they had both fallen asleep, and had explained to one another the events of the evening.

Kari took another look at Rom's bracelet. "So, basically, the staff comes out, you hit things with it and they die," she oversimplified.

"Well, it's not *that* easy," she muttered. "But, I guess, yeah. And I can jump really, really far."

"You already did that," Kari observed, thinking back to Rom's exploits in the orphanage.

"No, I can jump over *buildings* now!"

"No!"

"Yes," Rom blushed.

"Truly?"

"*Truly.*"

Kari's jaw dropped. "That's wonderful!"

Rom grinned. "It kind of is," she confessed.

Mulligan looked up from his small bowl of fruit to observe the two girls. His whiskers flicked randomly and he resumed eating.

"And all that music you were hearing," Rom asked, "that was Art?"

Kari nodded cheerfully.

"That's really strange. But at least you don't have a glowing purple thing in your head."

"I think it's beautiful!" Kari protested. "It makes you look like an angel. It's like, I can only hear Art. But you *are* Art."

Rom stubbornly tried not to agree, but secretly she did think it was rather wonderful. The thoughts of the millipede as it died clung to her, tainting the image of the angel as Kari described it – from the harvester to the reaper. She sighed, concealing the expression by taking a mouthful of food.

After they cleaned up from breakfast, Briseida walked the girls through the basics of operating the shop – from prices to what sorts of things were which, how to lock the door and set the wards. About an hour after they had opened the apothecary for business, three people came into the shop, all three wearing grayish-blue long coats with a copper-colored patch on the left lapel.

The patches were all the same – a complex arrangement of gears in a roughly triangular pattern, with the two moons and the sun at the corners. Kari recognized it instantly.

"You're from the college of Atmology!" Kari screamed, quite a bit louder than she would have liked, were she to have the chance to do it over.

The two men and the woman smiled kindly, nodding. The older gentleman – whose scant remaining hair was solid grey and long, sticking out at random intervals – bowed cordially at the waist.

"We are indeed, Miss," he said. Looking at them both and finally at Briseida, he added, "We are here to see a potential by the name of … Kari, is it?"

Kari jumped up, once before she could stop herself. "That's me!" she said excitedly.

Briseida put her hands on Kari's shoulders. "Yes, dear, these are the people I said would be here to speak with you today. Please escort them into the guest's parlor, would you?" She tightened her grip only slightly, adding, "And please do try not to bring the building down in your enthusiasm."

Kari bit her lip. "I'll try," she half-grinned.

* * * * *

She showed the three scientists into the other room, leaving Briseida and Rom alone in the shop. Briseida took the opportunity to watch Rom as Rom alternated her gaze between the direction Kari and the others had gone and staring vacantly out the front window.

"You're too worried," the young woman said. "What troubles you?"

"What's gonna happen?" Rom said. "Everything's going to change. Kari's going to go off to school now, and I'm some kind of weird girl who fights monsters, and the first night I'm here people break into the shop…"

Briseida listened to her silently as Rom continued.

"And I've got Mully – and I do like you, Mully, I really do – but it's kind of weird that he can talk, and there's a bad lady who's also like me and she wants to kill me or take my soul or something, and I don't know what to do about that either…" She took a deep breath and was going to go on, but she thought better of it. "It's just not fair," was all she said.

"What's not fair?"

Rom scrunched up her mouth. "Well, Kari's going to be like the best steamsmith ever or something, Cousins...well, he's Cousins, I guess. He knows just about everyone, and almost everyone likes him." She leaned over the counter and rested her cheek on her arm while she scratched Mully's fur. "Everybody's smart, and all I can do is break things."

Mulligan looked up at Briseida and tilted his head to the back office. She smiled and nodded. "Rom, dear, I don't want to lie to you. I don't have the answers you need right now. I know you're a wonderful girl, and I think you're absolutely clever. I think things aren't quite how you think they are, but I also think that you do have a lot more to offer than just breaking things."

"Like what?"

Briseida looked down at the grey-furred feranzanthum and caught his eyes. He nodded slightly.

Mulligan shrugged off Rom's hand. "I'm glad you asked," he said. "Let's go sit down someplace comfortable, and I'll tell you a few things I've started remembering."

"Remembering?"

He shrugged, his small batlike wings flapping several times. "Memory put a lot of things in my head – more things than a little thing like me should have to know. It takes a little while to sort them out," he explained.

"Besides…" his voice trailed off.

A strange discomfort was starting to build in Rom's stomach. She looked sharply towards the general direction of the fields. "Do you –"

He nodded. "I feel it, too."

She was already running towards the door by the time Mulligan was able to perch on her shoulder. "Bree!" she called back as she left the shop. "Tell Kari I'm going to the fields!"

Briseida watched as the girl and her small guardian animal ran down the street and turned a corner, out of sight. It was as the old books said of the Sheharid Is'iin, she thought to herself. *Always in motion, rarely resting. Like the bees in the garden, like the hummingbirds, like the thunder from the sky.*

Chapter 19: The Mundaline

In the morning, Cousins and Ian had already left, leaving Rom and Kari alone to help Briseida with breakfast and the morning chores. Rom and Kari had spoken until they had both fallen asleep, and had explained to one another the events of the evening.

Kari took another look at Rom's bracelet. "So, basically, the staff comes out, you hit things with it and they die," she oversimplified.

"Well, it's not *that* easy," she muttered. "But, I guess, yeah. And I can jump really, really far."

"You already did that," Kari observed, thinking back to Rom's exploits in the orphanage.

"No, I can jump over *buildings* now!"

"No!"

"Yes," Rom blushed.

"Truly?"

"*Truly.*"

Kari's jaw dropped. "That's wonderful!"

Rom grinned. "It kind of is," she confessed.

Mulligan looked up from his small bowl of fruit to observe the two girls. His whiskers flicked randomly and he resumed eating.

"And all that music you were hearing," Rom asked, "that was Art?"

Kari nodded cheerfully.

"That's really strange. But at least you don't have a glowing purple thing in your head."

"I think it's beautiful!" Kari protested. "It makes you look like an angel. It's like, I can only hear Art. But you *are* Art."

Rom stubbornly tried not to agree, but secretly she did think it was rather wonderful. However, the thoughts of the millipede as it had died clung to her, tainting the image of the angel as Kari described it – turning her image of herself from the harvester to the reaper. She sighed, concealing the expression by taking a mouthful of food.

After they cleaned up from breakfast, Briseida walked the girls through the basics of operating the shop – from prices to what sorts of things were which, how to lock the door and set the wards. About an hour after they had opened the apothecary for business, three people came into the shop, all three wearing grayish-blue long coats with a copper-colored patch on the left lapel.

The patches were all the same – a complex arrangement of gears in a roughly triangular pattern, with the two moons and the sun at the corners. Kari recognized it instantly.

"You're from the college of Atmology!" Kari screamed, quite a bit louder than she would have liked, were she to have the chance to do it over.

The two men and the woman smiled kindly, nodding. The older gentleman – whose scant remaining hair was solid grey and long, sticking out at random intervals – bowed cordially at the waist.

"We are indeed, Miss," he said. Looking at them both and finally at Briseida, he added, "We are here to see a potential by the name of … Hikari, is it?"

Kari jumped up, once before she could stop herself. "That's me!" she said excitedly.

Briseida put her hands on Kari's shoulders. "Yes, dear, these are the people I said would be here to speak with you today. Please escort them into the guest's parlor, would you?" She tightened her grip only slightly, adding, "And please do try not to bring the building down in your enthusiasm."

Kari bit her lip. "I'll try," she half-grinned.

She showed the three scientists into the other room, leaving Briseida and Rom alone in the shop. Briseida took the opportunity to watch Rom as Rom alternated her gaze between the direction Kari and the others had gone and staring vacantly out the front window.

"You're too worried," the young woman said. "What troubles you?"

"What's gonna happen?" Rom said. "Everything's going to change. Kari's going to go off to school now, and I'm some kind of weird girl who fights monsters, and the first night I'm here people break into the shop…"

Briseida listened to her silently as Rom continued.

"And I've got Mully – and I do like you, Mully, I really do – but it's kind of weird that he can talk, and there's a bad lady who's also like me and she wants to kill me or take my soul or something, and I don't know what to do about that either…" She took a deep breath and was going to go on, but she thought better of it. "It's just not fair," was all she said.

"What's not fair?"

Rom scrunched up her mouth. "Well, Kari's going to be like the best steamsmith ever or something, Cousins...well, he's Cousins, I guess. He knows just about everyone, and almost everyone likes him." She leaned over the counter and rested her cheek on her arm while she scratched Mully's fur. "Everybody's smart, and all I can do is break things."

Mulligan looked up at Briseida and tilted his head to the back office. She smiled and nodded. "Rom, dear, I don't want to lie to you. I don't have the answers you need right now. I know you're a wonderful girl, and I think you're absolutely clever. I think things aren't quite how you think they are, but I also think that you do have a lot more to offer than just breaking things."

"Like what?"

Briseida looked down at the grey-furred feranzanthum and caught his eyes. He nodded slightly.

Mulligan shrugged off Rom's hand. "I'm glad you asked," he said. "Let's go sit down someplace comfortable, and I'll tell you a few things I've started remembering."

"Remembering?"

He shrugged, his small batlike wings flapping several times. "Memory put a lot of things in my head – more things than a little thing like me should have to know. It takes a little while to sort them out," he explained.

"But there is a lot you're going to have to learn, and you aren't going to have as much time to learn it as you want. So she gave me a lot of information to help you. Like what you can do, what you will be able to do, and what you have to do. There's a lot more going on than you realize, but Memory knows that you are much stronger than you know, too. Besides..." his voice trailed off.

A strange discomfort was starting to build in Rom's stomach. She looked sharply towards the general direction of the fields, and held up a hand to interrupt him. "Do you –"

He nodded, sighing. "I feel it, too."

She was already running towards the door by the time Mulligan was able to perch on her shoulder. "Bree!" she called back as she left the shop. "Tell Kari I'm going to the fields!"

Briseida watched as the girl and her small guardian animal ran down the street and turned a corner, out of sight. It was as the old books said of the Sheharid Is'iin, she thought to herself. *Always in motion, rarely resting. Like the bees in the garden, like the hummingbirds, like the lightning in the sky.*

Chapter 19: The Mundaline

Still two streets from the fields, Rom knew her sense was right – the workers were running past her in a chaotic stream, more than one bloodied and obviously injured. After being run into for the third time, she took a deep breath and jumped up and onto the nearest rooftop. From there, she took another relatively small jump, and then another, until she landed just near the edge of the final building towards the fields.

A small gathering of workers seemed focused on something not too far from the city itself – they were clustered in a loose circle, and something large and blue moved quickly among them. Screams and calls for help made their way to her ears. She tapped the bracelet and summoned her shepherd's crook.

"Hold on tight, this is a long jump," she said. Mulligan complied.

She kicked off, and the winds rustled through the folds and pleated gathers of the dress – only the sound of the fabric and the wind whistling past them could be heard until she landed, just beyond the men. Her big black boots dug into the soil, cutting a pair of uneven furrows until she came to a stop.

"Run!" she yelled to the men. "Go on, I'll take care of this!"

A few of them were reluctant to leave this young white-haired girl – particularly, the ones who did not see her just leap more than a hundred feet across the sky – but enough did so to give her a clear view of the indigo-furred creature.

It was taller than her at its shoulders, with a black and matted mane and a single horn extending upwards from the tip of his nose. It had the look of a large dog, but with pointed ears and enormous bird's wings protruding from its back. Its tail was long and flicking about, the end barbed with what looked to be a large assortment of quills.

"A mundaline," Mulligan whispered. "They're… really tough," he said, falling substantially short of the mark for his efforts at nonchalance, but overcompensating as he continued, "but I'm sure you'll best him."

"Thanks," she said dryly. "I feel much better now."

She slapped the staff into the palm of her hand. "Hey, you! Big blue dog-cat-thing!" It fixed his attention on her and she began to back away slowly, drawing it away from the group of farmers. They opened the circle into a large curving line, standing as if to defend the city against this wild beast.

"Come on, you whatever you are! Come on and fight me!"

"You're doing great, Rom, he's definitely doing exactly what you're telling him to do."

"Hush, Mully," she hissed.

"Do you have a plan for this?" he asked nervously.

"A plan for what?" She twirled the staff around a few times to keep its attention on her – the whistling sound created as the curved top cut through the air seemed to work.

His whisper increased in intensity. "What do you mean, a plan for what?"

She sighed. "You need to figure something out about me, Mully."

"What's that?"

She stopped moving backwards, and placed one foot back behind her, turning partially away from the creature and holding her staff in one hand, the top pointed low towards the ground. The mundaline paused, lowering itself towards the ground.

"I *never* plan things out," she said with a smile.

The beast jumped straight towards her, claws flashing in the morning sun. Rom dove to one side, letting it pass her. The mundaline's speed was astonishing; even prepared for its leap, Rom only missed having its claws disembowel her by a hand's-breadth. And just as she was about to mentally congratulate herself for her cleverness, its tail smacked into her right leg, sending an instant shock of fiery pain along her side.

She tried to turn with the impact, but even as the creature landed and prepared for a second pass, she felt the tug of its tail as it pulled free. Looking down as quickly as she dared, she could see five or six barbed quills emerging from her dress, firmly impaled into her thigh. A strong burning sensation suggested to her that they were tipped in some kind of venom.

"Oh, that's not good," she grumbled, taking a quick hop-step back and bringing her crook up defensively. Her right leg throbbed; the muscles were shivering in response to the constant painful irritation of the quills.

"What's not?" Mulligan looked quickly down. "Oh," he remarked. "Yes, that's not good."

"I'm open for ideas," she said, jumping again as the mundaline pounced again. This time, however, she was ready and batted the tail away as it flicked her direction.

"You're sure?" her small friend remarked, impossibly capable of faint sarcasm even in the midst of a life and death crisis. "I wouldn't want to introduce a hint of forethought into a strategy that thus far..."

"Mully, I'm serious!" she interrupted, diving again, this time to the right. Her right leg was growing stiff; her last dodge was close enough that the mundaline's claws caught on one of the pleats of her dress, tearing a small gash through the black fabric.

"Okay, okay, but this is what I've been trying to tell you," he said, his voice rising slightly in timbre as he struggled to hold on to her shoulders. "You always jump in without thinking ahead..."

"*Not now!*" Rom snapped. Bracing herself on her left foot, she raised the crook and caught the mundaline in the neck as it tried to leap at her again. The thickly matted fur of its mane blunted the blow, however, but forced the creature to rethink its strategy nonetheless. It shook its head angrily, and flapped its wings once, sending up a brief gust of wind against Rom. The blast of air blew her dress, pulling at the quills that remained in her leg, causing her to wince again at the pain. It felt as if the entire region was split open and being prodded by dozens of tiny teeth.

"Sorry, Rom, I'm thinking of something," Mulligan offered. He wanted to suggest taking a moment to remove the quills before they did any further damage, but there was no way to do that while the mundaline remained active. And while the mundaline seemed sick, it was still much stronger and almost as fast as Rom, while her injury was rapidly impacting her ability to fight. He knew that the mundalines normally attacked from the air when they felt their homes were threatened, but fought on the ground when hunting smaller prey. That realization didn't make him feel any better about the situation.

There was something oddly familiar to Rom about the mundaline's manner of pacing. It was almost like the alley cats that occasionally frequented the streets of Oldtown, but there was a manner of its eye contact that made her think back to the wild dogs she'd run across as a child.

Taking an opportunity to strike while the mundaline seemed to be patiently waiting for the quills' venom to do its work, Rom thrust the crook out at its furthest reach. The large curved end smacked the mundaline smartly across the nose. The result was surprising; the mundaline jumped back, blinking its eyes and shaking its head fiercely.

"What are you doing, Rom?"

Rom ignored his question, instead raising her voice imperially to the large blue creature. "Bad mundaline!" she said curtly. "Bad!"

The mundaline responded with a pair of sneezes, triggered by the bat on the tip of its snout, and cocked its head to one side, evidently confused by its prey's response. Rom continued fierce eye contact with the beast, gritting her teeth and maintaining her crook extended towards its nose. To Mully, she directed, "Climb down and pull out the needles, quickly!"

With a nod of his head, Mulligan dropped down to hang from the belted sash on her waist and tentatively pulled on one of the thin quills.

Rom hissed in pain. "Don't just pull on them; pull them *out*!" She had to move to the left in a sequence of careful steps as the mundaline began to pace again, growling deeply in its chest. She jabbed with the crook again to make it reconsider; it paused, but started back the predatory circle towards Rom's left side.

Mulligan yanked the first of the quills free, nearly causing Rom to drop the crook in the shock of the flash of pain that tore through her. The mundaline prepared to leap again, but she jabbed a warning thrust of the crook at its nose again, forcing it to flinch backwards.

The two pivoted around one another for several protracted moments, while Mulligan methodically plucked the barbed quills from Rom's leg. By the time he was done, blood trails crisscrossed her right leg and her toes felt sticky inside the boot.

As Mulligan began to climb back up onto Rom's shoulder, the mundaline pounced again, forcing Rom to jump straight up. She kicked off from the ground intuitively, but caught Mulligan mid-climb, sending him tumbling to the ground. He rolled into a ball, landing just behind the mundaline's front paws.

The monster dug his claws into the soil, however, and followed Rom's path over his head, his tremendous jaws wide open and yellowed fangs sparkling with tainted saliva. Seeing this, the young Reaper swung the crook ahead of her jump and down into a powerful strike against the crown of its skull with a loud *thwok*. The strike gave her leverage against her own jump, bolstering her angle and dropping her several meters out of range of its barbed tail.

Her right leg gave out on the landing; Rom tried to counter for this and failed, sprawling face-first into the ground.

Her ears rang, but she could hear Mulligan's voice cutting through the dizziness. "Rom!"

She rolled over, whipping the crook in a defensive arc which struck the mundaline as it tried to land atop her. So powerful was the strike that it made her whole arm shudder, but managed to knock the beast over onto its side. Rom got to her feet as quickly as she could. The wounds from the barbs didn't sting as much anymore, but her leg was clearly not enthusiastically supportive of all Rom's intended exertions.

The creature's eyes flashed red and darted back and forth between Rom and Mulligan, as if deciding between the meal and a snack. Rom spun the crook over her head, hoping again that the high-pitched whine the motion produced would keep the mundaline's attention focused on her.

But at that moment, Mulligan whistled briskly and launched himself high into the air with a burst of his wings. The mundaline responded with a mighty flap of his own wings, flying off after the much-smaller feranzanthum. Rom gasped, and tried to jump up as well, but her right leg flinched at the last moment, and she fell far past her target.

She stood, helpless, watching the two animals soar high into the sky above her, and tried to remember to breathe.

Chapter 20: Finding Allies Among the Dead

The brilliance of the sky embraced the tranquility of the voluminous rounded clouds above Oldtown. In any other situation it might have been a breathtakingly beautiful day for flying. Being chased for one's life by a rabid undead monster took some of the awe out of the moment, however.

He'd somehow managed to stay ahead of his pursuer until reaching the obscuring cloudbanks, but they blinded him as much as he hoped it blinded the mundaline. His efforts at aerial camouflage were hampered by the fact that the flapping of his wings weren't entirely silent. Fearing being snuck up on by an aggressive predatory dive, Mulligan had to frequently break into the open sky, attempt to discern the location of the other creature and then slip back under the cloak of the cloud cover.

Principal among his thoughts were attempting to buy Rom time to heal up. *Her enhanced metabolism should handle the toxins of the needles*, he reasoned, but it would still be several minutes more before she was back to her full strength.

A faint whistling was all the warning he had; he drew in his wings at once and dropped like a small stone as the much larger mundaline dove past him. Mully shot his right wing out for an instant, sending him into a full roll to the left, just barely avoiding a quill-laden tail swipe.

I'm not designed for this sort of combat! He thought. *Maybe if I get much larger, or when my horns grow in, perhaps, but for now all I have is being small and adorable. Not to mention being more clever than the average undead monster,* he amended.

He was forced to concede that all the brains in the world might not help if the mundaline sank its claws into him. A shiver cascaded across his fur from crown to tail, and not from the chill in the moist-filled cloudbanks. He ducked again, shaking his head at the near miss. *Ready or not, here we come,* he thought, pulling his wings in tightly and forming a Mulligan-shaped spear, letting gravity work its own magic upon him. It had only been a few minutes; Rom was unlikely to be completely healed up, but whatever condition she was in, it would have to be enough.

The clouds spat him out, a thin trail of mist marking his passage straight down towards the ground. Though his eyes were mostly squinted against the stinging wind, he glanced up briefly – from his current vantage point, he was higher than the Wall; he could see into the gleaming spires of Aesirium beyond. Whether it was a trick of the light or the moisture in his eyes, the light seemed to be in motion up and along the needle-shaped towers. Motion? Movement? He mentally shrugged. Mulligan conceded that it was one mystery that was only a matter of time in the solving. With Rom's temperament, no secret was safe from her unhinged curiosity.

The tree line was a broad green stroke across the landscape beneath him; the mundaline had chased him a bit about the clouds, and Mulligan had to make a series of small adjustments to ensure he returned to his original location in the fields below. He dare not look behind him, as much as he wanted to. The noise of the wind was so great that he couldn't hear if the Mundaline was chasing him, so he held his course and speed. After all, he reasoned, it was all he could do. If the mundaline managed to catch him, there wasn't much he could do about it now, anyway.

"He's been gone too long," Rom said to nobody in particular. The farmers were standing a good ways off still, while the strange young white-haired girl with the purple gem paced back and forth. Every few moments, she would stop and stare up into the sky for a sign, a shadow, a bit of evidence that Mully was all right. Suddenly, her eyes were drawn to a small dot, descending rapidly. Rom sheltered her eyes with one hand to try and see it more clearly, gasping in fear when she realized it was the mundaline diving towards her, and not Mulligan. A low growl rose in her chest. The pain in her leg was instantly forgotten.

It had tilted back its wings, and seemed to be gaining in speed as it approached – Rom imagined she could see its snarling maw from her position on the ground, and she tried to guess how many more seconds would pass before he was here. The additional thought occurred to her: *going that fast, he's really going to hurt me.* She lifted the crook up over her shoulder, holding it firmly in both hands like the children on the streets did when playing stickball.

Her heart raced. She couldn't remember feeling this scared. For that matter, it was hard to remember ever feeling scared at all. But just now, staring up at the rapidly approaching feral mundaline, Rom realized that she was terrified.

It was coming so fast; would she be able to hit it? It was practically a blur now; she could hear a high-pitched whistle of the wind streaking past its falling body. Could she swing the staff quickly enough? Could she dodge it? She considered how slow she must be in comparison to its blinding descent. I'm not fast enough, she realized. I'm not fast enough...

Even as she watched, her hands tightly wound around the mystically powerful staff, she felt the air grow thick around her. The hairs on the back of her neck stood straight out, and her mouth went dry. Even as she watched, the mundaline was slowing down; she could see it, she was certain, now. He still seemed to be moving at an extraordinary rate of speed, with the dark blue hair nearly flattened against his face and body, wings drawn back to guide him in with the fury of a lightning bolt.

And right there, only an arm's breadth ahead of him, was Mully.

She nearly screamed with delight, but realized she only had moments to act. They both seemed to be moving more slowly, but still steadily towards her. Rom reached out with the crook, and aimed it for the underside of the mundaline's jaw, and held out her hand towards Mulligan.

In the last possible second, she wedged the base of the crook into the ground and aimed the broad, curving end against the mundaline as she pulled Mulligan away and threw them both to the ground and out of the mundaline's reach.

They hit the soil and there was a loud crack indicating the collision between the mundaline and the crook. Rom rolled back up onto her feet, holding Mulligan securely in her arms. She blinked – it must have been her imagination, because everything seemed back to normal now. Absently, her hand brushed the pocket of her black dress which held the oddly-comforting silver watch. A coolness she briefly felt there set the hairs on her arm to standing.

A cloud of dust and dirt had filled the air. Waving it quickly away with one hand, Rom saw her shepherd's crook and picked it up. She nodded appreciatively in that it seemed no worse for wear.

"Be careful, Rom," Mulligan cautioned. "He's tough and clever."

"I know," she said. Beyond the dust, she could see it now, rising unsteadily back up onto its feet. The impact had clearly injured him, but he wasn't done yet. It shook its head and tried to growl, but coughed out a quantity of dark green matter onto the soil.

Seeing Rom, however, it bared its fangs and jumped at her again.

Rom sprung in a hands-free cartwheel out of its path, her staff arcing up and around to loop around the end of its tail. As he landed past her, she stood quickly and pulled hard on the staff, tearing the remainder of the quills free.

The creature howled and spun quickly on the girl – she timed her jump as it charged her perfectly and brought the bottom of the staff down on its head and vaulted out of its reach to land behind it.

"You're just making him angry," Mulligan observed.

"Sorry. I'm still getting the hang of – whoops – this," she said, springing again out of its way as it doubled back towards her.

"Still waiting for a plan," Mulligan mentioned.

"Hush! Distracting me."

It half-leaped at her again, but then turned abruptly, catching her as she had tried to dodge him, and pinning her to the ground. She had just barely managed to pull her staff up to catch beneath his paws, keeping his claws from slicing her open. Its fetid breath stank of old socks and an open sewer.

"Sorry about this," she winced, drawing her boots up beneath him and kicking him hard in the stomach. The force of the kick sent him flying, off balance, to land several feet away. They were both on their feet at once, but with Rom looking much better off in terms of injuries.

The impact of landing upside down from her powerful kick appeared to have injured one of his wings, which was now folded in an obviously abnormal direction.

"Oh, no, I'm so sorry," she said sincerely. The demeanor of the beast seemed different now, as well. He was pacing nervously, as if confused by the painful shock of his broken wing. The farmers seemed to notice this as well, and let out a loud cheer. They ran closer, holding up their field tools. Rom had seen the tools many times before – this was the first time she had ever realized they made effective weapons. But she knew that all too often the wounded beasts were the most deadly.

She held up the staff between herself and the oncoming farmers. "Stay back," she commanded. To her surprise, they listened. Looking back at the creature, she could see something distinctly changed in his eyes.

"Mully?" she said. "Something's happened to it."

"I see it too," he said.

"I think it's going to be okay."

Mulligan looked askance at his Sheharid pupil. "You have a plan, finally?"

"I'm going to try and talk to him."

He blinked. "Whoa, wait, Rom. Not all of us 'monsters' actually speak, you know."

"He does."

"Are you sure? I'm not that familiar with them, I don't — that is…Oh, I think I get it."

She was close enough now that he could have easily attacked her, but he did not. She held up her staff in one hand, but extended to the side. "Easy, you big… you… well, *you*. Just relax."

To her and Mully's surprise, the creature nodded.

"Can you speak?" she asked him.

The creature opened its mouth, but no sound came out – instead, it turned to one side and began to cough violently. The coughing fit eventually seemed to pass, but the animal's breath was ragged and came in short and obviously painful gasps. The effort seemed to have drained the last of his strength, however; his legs trembled and then buckled, and he collapsed to the ground heavily. As she approached him, he shook his head, and then his eyes looked from her to focus specifically on the gem in her forehead. It took one last, trembling breath, and released it in a deep sigh.

Rom could hear him, almost, in her mind. She felt him as a young cub through adulthood, learning to hunt and to fly, eventually assuming the duties of the leader of his tribe. Then the fires came, engulfing nearly all who he was sworn to protect; the other males, the females and the cubs. The others became corrupted, monstrous, some sort of rotting creations, mindless and feral. One by one, he hunted these unholy things down that had once been part of his own tribe and slew them. And then the burning in his own heart and mind began to consume him. The last thoughts of this magnificent creature were of profound regret, knowing that in the end, there had been none of his tribe left to mercifully end his life.

The body remained completely still for another heartbeat, and then Rom could feel a sense that the life was at last leaving him. She thought her eyes were playing tricks – a thin fluttering wisp, like the faintest puff of steam, rose up from his form and hung there against the breeze for one final second before vanishing entirely. Rom couldn't explain what caused her to do so, but with the last movement of the great beast, she fell to her knees and wept.

She cried until her head hurt, until it felt as if it would split from the ferocity of her sorrow, until she felt a depth of calmness and tranquility rise up from the depths of her melancholia and embrace her like a long-lost sibling. A peace caressed her heart, and her tears were stilled, drying on her cheeks.

* * *

Mulligan walked up behind her, and hopped up onto her shoulders, purring softly. He had noticed that such gestures seemed particularly pleasant to people; he assumed it had something to do with the musical elements inherent to the vibration, but whatever the reason, it seemed effective.

The farmers kindly kept their distance for several minutes, eventually moving up and offering to move the body away and dispose of it.

She was going to protest, but then realized that they'd stopped talking and were instead staring at her face in silence and shock. Mulligan leaned back to examine her face, too, and his eyes as well widened.

"Rom," he breathed.

"What is it, Mully?" she said, wiping her nose with the back of her hand.

"You have a new gem."

She flinched. "Another one?" Her hand rose to her forehead – sure enough, there was a second gem – though the first one seemed to have split into two, and now both gems were evenly spaced across her skin. The new gem felt warm to the touch – and no sooner had she touched it as there was a bright flash of blue light that caused all the men to jump back in fear.

And when the light faded, there stood before her a shimmering, semi-translucent mundaline. It was the same size and shape, but where it had been a dark indigo only moments before, it now fairly shone a deep bright blue of a summer day. It looked about, fixed his eyes on her, and bowed.

"Mistress Rom", it said, its voice a sturdy baritone. "I pledge my life to you in service. May I repay in death the wrongs I have committed in life."

"W-wait," she stammered. "What - - are you asking me?" She looked at Mully, then back to the creature. "What *ARE* you asking me?"

"I believe he's asking-"

The creature cut him off. "I am giving my life to you to do with as you will. I will remain with you, if you please, to call forth if you have need."

"Oh," Mulligan said. "That's what I thought," he lied.

The farmers stood as one and appeared to see Rom in a new way. She heard them whisper among themselves – and heard the word "Reaper" and "Harvester" mentioned more than once.

"How do I tell him it's okay?" she whispered, feeling intensely self-conscious all of a sudden. She just wanted to figure out the quickest way to make them all stop looking at her.

"You want him to go away?"

The creature took another step forward, flexing his great black wings and stirring up a small cloud of dust around them. "Please, Mistress Rom," it said, his voice softer, "I beg of you to give me a chance to earn back my honor, lost as I was in the actions of my delusional self."

"You... promise to behave?" she asked.

He again lowered his head. "I do so swear."

"Very well," she said. "I accept. Just... you're really ... big. And we don't have a lot of space for you where we live."

He seemed to smile; she couldn't be certain. "Thus I shall return, through your gem."

"You *live* ...in there?"

He nodded. "My soul remains in that way connected to life by your grace."

"Wow." She blinked. "That's really ..." She couldn't think of the right word, so she let silence capture it.

He bowed again. "When you have need, call forth and Yu will appear."

Her forehead wrinkled, confused. "I will appear?"

"No. *I* will appear."

"But you said I will appear," she repeated, clearly confused.

He laughed; a low, gentle sound. "I called myself by the name given to me by the keeper of my spirit: Yu."

"Oh!" she giggled. "You're *Yu*! Your name is Yu!"

"I am Yu," he agreed.

She laughed again. "Okay, Yu. You go on back, and I'll see Yu later. You. Yu." She giggled again, and he laughed softly as well, bowing again and vanishing in another burst of purple light.

Mully shook his head, pondering his role as guardian animal to this obviously deranged little girl.

"Oh yes, that joke's – *never* – going to get old."

Rom remained in the fields for several hours; fearful that the creature's decaying body would draw the wrath of additional predators, they collected a small pile of wild underbrush and dragged the body atop it, and set it ablaze. Although the men would not let her assist, she stood by the burning pyre until long after it had turned to ash, left relatively alone in her thoughts.

As she distantly watched the men leave, she observed the change in how they looked at her. Not two days ago, she, the impoverished and parentless child in tatters, would have been all but ignored by them – a sad reminder of the harsh realities of their world. She had been very much like the Wall which kept them all apart from the wondrous life of the True Citizens of the city beyond: always present, but generally ignored. When she had been younger, she had asked one of the Matrons why they didn't talk about the Wall, why they never tried to climb it, search for a door – why they hadn't heard from anyone inside the Wall in so many years and yet never thought to find out why?

The Matron told her, "Kicking the Wall will not bring it down." It hadn't made sense to her, but it was all the Matron would say in response; and, after asking too many times, Rom was sent to the bathroom to help clean.

"Mully, is this how it's always going to be?" she asked. "I'm just going to fight things and have to kill them?"

"No," he whispered. "Something was wrong with him. He didn't die from the fight, I think he was already dying when we got here."

She nodded softly. "I…as he was dying, I saw it, saw who he was, and all the things that happened to him and his pack. Something made them all sick, like him."

"It wasn't natural, whatever it was," Mully said. "There was an artificial corruption to his breath – some foul smell about it."

"Yes, I thought so, too!" Rom scratched Mully's head. "Is that some other thing I can do, as a Sheharid?"

"It's part of who you are," he said. "You are a guardian over life and death - - so I think you can feel when death is approaching something – or has already come."

She looked in the opposite direction from the city, out into the wild. "There's something out there, Mully. Something that's been making the animals crazy. Ian said it himself; there have been more of them coming into the city than ever before."

"You think something's happening to them?"

Rom was quiet for a long moment, listening to the urging of her spirit.

"No, not something," she said. "Some*one*."

Chapter 21: Answers and Questions

Kari stood at the door of the shop, waving merrily to the professors as they left. She closed the door and practically skipped back to the counter and Briseida.

"They were so nice! And smart!" her eyes were wide as she spoke. "They said I can start my instruction next week, even though it's in the middle of a term, and they're going to assign me my own private tutor so I can catch up with the other apprentices, and they're even going to let me work in my very own workshop in the labs if I want and OH wow I really really want to and..." she paused long enough to look around the room. "Where's Rom?"

She spun about twice before Briseida was able to tell her. "She and Mulligan had to go, there was something... she had to do. She went to the fields," she said.

Kari frowned. "I wanted to tell her about my meeting," she pouted.

"I'm sure she'll be back soon, dear. Why don't you help me with the shop until she gets back?"

The young girl nodded, but did so absently. Her moment of celebration, as wonderful as it was, simply wasn't as good without her friend here to share it.

As if in answer to her wish, Rom returned a moment later, walking slowly with Mulligan on her shoulder. She entered the shop, saw Kari and made her way over to her friend. Without saying a word, she gave Kari a long hug.

"Are you okay, Rom?"

Rom nodded softly and stepped away. "Everything's changing so quickly," she said quietly. "Just look at what's happened just in the last couple days. I'm just worried what'll happen next."

Kari's dark eyes rose to Rom's forehead. "Oh!"

Affecting a self-conscious smile, Rom nodded. "Two." The two girls laughed at the memory.

"And I have another friend, kind of like Mully, but he's up here," she said, pointing again to her forehead. "He's a mundaline."

"What's a mundaline?"

Rom shrugged. "Dunno. But he's one. I'd show you, but he's kind of, um, large. How was your day?"

Kari bit her lip. "Ummm…" she started.

"Oh wait! Your interview! How was it? Did they see how brilliant you are?" Rom instantly felt guilty for her selfish worries, and tried to make up for it by focusing on Kari's circumstances.

"It was really great," Kari said, her own enthusiasm picking back up. "They said I'm going to be one of the youngest apprentices in the whole college!"

Rom's smile was sincere, beaming for the opportunities for her friend. She'd always thought Kari was smart, but it was great to see Kari getting the kind of recognition Rom believed her friend deserved.

Other concerns abandoned in their happy conversation, the two girls left the shop, fluttering fragments of their words filling the empty spaces of the old building.

Briefly pausing while mixing an ointment that guarded against rust-spawned infections, Briseida smiled at the relative resilience of the young spirit – she'd seen both girls, momentarily saddened, revive instantly at the reappearance of the other. And if what Goya suggested that the old tomes predicted for these two girls was even remotely accurate, they would need that collaborative support more than they could possibly imagine. She sighed softly, choosing instead to busy herself with the sort of mundane tasks that she did have some power over, rather than dwelling upon potential eventualities which she did not.

Upstairs, Cousins sat in a small study on the east side of the building, staring out across Oldtown through his Looking Glasses. He'd uncovered over a dozen separate filter combinations to the goggles, and was scanning through them, rolling the tiny adjustment dials across their full breadth, methodically exploring the way they would help him see the world.

Many of the settings were fairly straightforward, but of them all, one had caught his fancy most curiously. Where the other dials, when adjusted to their extreme, simply cycled back to the initial settings, one particular gear stopped after spinning it to a certain point. At first, when he spun the dial, he thought it was shimmering like starlight; but as he dialed the gear more slowly he realized he was seeing around him in days and nights. A broader adjustment showed him snow upon the ground, then back to spring and summer. His heart pounded in his chest; these were impressive glasses indeed, he realized.

But when the dial reached its furthest end, his breath caught in his throat. For when he looked out upon the world at its most expanded view, the mighty Wall, the impenetrable symbol of their town's exile, was gone.

Where it had once stood was at that point nothing more than rubble; and beyond it... nothing.

Cousins continued to look for several moments, but at last dialed the Looking Glasses back to their original settings, and removed them from his eyes, sliding them up onto his forehead. For more than an hour, he sat, staring out at the Wall, as consideration of the countless probabilities danced through his imagination.

Eventually, the sounds of laughter and the tantalizing smells of freshly-cooked dinner made their way to him, luring him from his thoughts and back downstairs to be among his new friends.

To be continued in Book 2 of the Chronicles of

Aesirium:

<u>The Morrow Stone</u>

Excerpt from Book Two of the Chronicles of

Aesirium:

THE MORROW STONE

Chapter 1: An Unscheduled Appointment

Cousins grabbed the small rise that lined the rooftop for balance, waiting for the nausea to pass. "You know, in spite of the warning," he said, taking a deep breath to calm his stomach, "that certainly was no amusement whatsoever."

Ian nodded. "My *Elsewhere* spell does take a certain degree of stamina," he confessed. "It will pass shortly, however."

The young man agreed, and sure enough in a few moments the feeling of vertigo left him. "You do that a great deal?"

"Only when speed is of the essence," came the reply. "Which building is Favo's?"

"The tall one," Cousins pointed. One building over from where they had arrived stood a towering edifice, four full stories tall with an additional structure built on the rooftop. To the casual observer, it would have appeared to be simply a taller building than the rest. But Cousins knew better.

At regular intervals on all the floors, there were narrow slits with angled openings – allowing defensive units to have a full view of the adjoining areas plus the street below, while offering limited opportunity for potential attacks. The overtly visible presence of security was limited – but just obvious enough to deter the casual thief.

The occasional glint of sunlight was additionally reflected off embedded stones within the brickwork, suggesting magically reinforced protection. He mentioned this to Ian, who confirmed it with a nod. "I can hear additional magical signatures coming from within the building as well," he said. "Favo is a man not only with great secrets, but with strong connections."

"That's true." Cousins looked around them, frowning again. "So what's our plan?"

Ian shrugged. "For now, the plan is to observe Favo, and attempt to discern his motives. Clearly he sought something held in Goya's shop, and most likely it is the Morrow Stone you delivered. But as to his motive or purpose, we have yet to determine."

"We're not going to determine anything from over here," Cousins grumbled. "He's too well defended."

"You have a suggestion?"

"Not really," the young man confessed. "A few fairly reckless ideas, but nothing worth mentioning. Regardless, I do think we should get off this rooftop – we're too obvious up here."

"I was just going to mention that myself," came a familiar female voice behind them. It was Molla, in a more casual outfit than the night before. She had a long jacket with long fur trim, and knee high brown leather boots with well-worn buckles. But the mask was gone, replaced by a pair of goggles worn high up on her head. Instead of the single holster she'd had last night, she had a twin holster rig, slung low across her hips. Both of the guns were drawn, one pointing at each of them.

For a fleeting moment, Cousins thought it might still be all right. She was one person, there were two of them; the numbers were still in their favor. But one by one, a half-dozen additional guards appeared around them from behind various points of concealment. He shook his head. If they'd been surprised by something mystical or magical, that would've at least been understandable, but they simply got out-maneuvered.

Molla and the guards escorted the two of them down the stairs in the center of the building and paraded them through the streets. The area around Favo's building wasn't too congested, but what few people were there moved quickly at the sight of Favo's guards, followed up by Molla herself. A few recognized Cousins, but not the tall gentleman who walked beside him. Regardless, they knew trouble when they saw it and they rarely kept looking at it when it was seen.

As they approached Favo's building, Cousins noticed a few people sitting around the area and engaged in apparently idle tasks – one woman folded the same piece of laundry multiple times; a man nearer the main entrance seemed to be taking forever to dislodge a pebble from his shoe – Cousins hid his smirk. Favo must be paranoid, he thought, to have undercover individuals outside his own building just for the purpose of, what, he wondered?

The main doorway was recessed into the main wall – there were two guards posted there, one at each side of the door, and nodded as Molla walked to the front of the procession. Two of the guards behind them peeled off in different directions, presumably to patrol the area, and the two at the head of the line opened the doors, allowing Molla to pass inside.

* * *

Cousins raised his arm to scratch an itch on his shoulder, eliciting a harsh rebuke from one of the guards. He held his hands back in front of him, apologizing. The guards pushed him from the back, driving him into the building. As the doors closed, the man in the courtyard slipped his boot onto his foot and walked casually away; a stack of laundry, abandoned, lingered in the late morning breeze.

The main floor followed a fairly uninteresting layout, Cousins thought. From a purely aesthetic perspective, it lacked artistry and décor; even in terms of basic human comforts, it was sorely lacking. He noted several regular square holes in the floor, however, and saw many solid oak panels with iron cross pieces leaning against nearby walls. He smiled. Favo was paranoid, he realized. The main floor was designed thus in order to provide a strong main floor defensive area; even should opposing forces manage to get past the impressively reinforced doors, they would face opponents on all quarters who could lay out defensive barriers at whatever interval or arrangement they liked. Cousins had to admit that although he didn't like Favo, he was starting to be impressed by him.

They took a partially-concealed stairway to the next floor, which was decorated more in line with his previous expectations. The main room consisted of a large central waiting area with mildly comfortable-looking chairs and a series of evenly spaced tables. Molla pointed to two of the chairs and told them to sit. Were a passerby not aware of the contingent of armed guards, they would never have known by Ian or Cousins' countenances that they were anything but honored guests, judging solely by their casual expressions.

Cousins even asked for water or tea, earning him a vicious look from Molla.

"Just stay here, Favo wants to speak to you." She turned and stepped through a pair of double doors at the opposite end of the room, and the four guards took positions around the room.

They could hear raised voices from the other side of the doors – most notably Molla's – and Ian glanced towards Cousins, the corner of his lips lifting in a smile so quick Cousins wasn't entirely certain he'd seen it. A moment later, the doors burst back open and there was Molla, her cheeks flushed with anger.

"Get in here," she snapped.

Again – only seeming to increase her frustration – the two stood casually and walked to the doors as if they had nothing more pressing on their minds. Molla nearly slammed the doors shut on Cousins as he stepped through.

Favo leaned against the edge of a large wooden desk and gestured towards two tall-backed leather covered chairs.

"Please, gentlemen, make yourselves comfortable. I hope you didn't have to wait long." He didn't have the appearance of a man whose name intimidated much of the city. He was slender, well dressed and with very fine shoes, Cousins noticed.

Ian nodded graciously. "No, your assistant made us feel quite at home. And it was really far too hot outside at any rate."

His polite disposition earned a tolerant smile from their host.

As they sat, Favo turned his attention to Cousins. "Well, my boy, you've been very busy, haven't you? Making a name for yourself, and without accepting my repeated offers of employment." He clucked his tongue. "Were I a lesser man, I might take umbrage at such effrontery." His charming smile belied the subtlety of his intentions.

Cousins matched him charm for charm. "Alas, such gentlemanly entrepreneurial and mutual respect is so rare," he said, letting his mouth savor the gliding intonations. "And yet," he added, "so valuable in its own right. Surely, you are a man of inestimable wealth."

"I do have the pair of coins to add music to my step, so to speak," Favo replied. His attention turned to Ian. "You, however, I do not know. You seem...familiar, but I cannot place you." He stood, pacing slowly and for dramatic effect. "Molla, surely you can place this man?"

She stepped around in front of them, staring intently at Ian's face. Glowering, she confessed, "No. He does look familiar, but I don't know from where."

Cousins' façade slipped. What were they playing at? They'd just seen him the night before in the shop, and yet here, the next day, they seemed genuinely confused as to who he was.

"It would appear I have one of those faces," Ian shrugged.

Favo circled the desk and sat in the large chair opposite his two guests. "Then perhaps you can explain why you were watching my building today?"

Ian glanced at Cousins, then looked back towards Favo. "We came to ask if you found what you were looking for last night."

Favo rolled his eyes dramatically. "You already know I did not. Not that it matters; I'm considering dropping the matter entirely."

Cousins and Ian ignored the obvious lie. Ian smiled. "Do you understand the nature of the item you have been paid to acquire, Favo?"

Turning towards Cousins, Favo shook his head. "Another 'cousin' of yours, then? Come all this way to attempt to sneak some information from me?"

He looked back at Ian. "I take care to ask few questions, beyond whether my clients are willing to pay what I want," he answered. Favo opened one of the drawers at the desk, pulled out a small bag, and shook it twice. He shrugged, and tossed it to Cousins. "That should pay off the old witch," he said. "And if you must know, I would have paid twice what they offered you if you had brought the item to me first."

Cousins nodded. "I'm certain you would have. But I can't reacquire my reputation for even *that* kind of money," he said.

Favo scoffed. "Ah, the peasant's honorable refuge. You would do well to reconsider your tolerance for those of us who don't stand up to your measure of ethics, Cousins. At some point, you may find yourself on the wrong side of a debt. Or worse."

Cousins stood up, placing the bag of coins in one of his many inner pockets. "That is some very intelligent advice, Favo. We're done for today, then?"

Ian sat a moment longer, then stood as well. Cousins noted a brief flash in Favo's eyes as they began to exit, but he filed it away to ask Ian later. Ian placed a hand on Cousins' shoulder and they moved towards the door. Molla stood between it and them until Favo waved her aside.

"You should come talk to me later, Cousins," he said. "You know I'll always have work for you. My door is always open."

Scowling, Molla stepped away and allowed them to leave. Two of the guards escorted them downstairs and out the front doors. They stood at the doorway until Ian and Cousins had walked out of sight.

A block away, Ian held out his hand.

"What?" Cousins asked.

Ian did not answer, merely pointed to the pocket where Cousins had placed the bag of coins and held out his hand again. Cousins released an exasperated sigh and handed it over.

"I was going to give it to her," he said.

Ian shook his head and dropped the bag into a bucket sitting beneath a water pump as they passed. The water in the bucket instantly began to boil, emitting a foul and acrid smoke.

Ian held Cousins by the arm and continued walking with him. "The bag contained a few tricks in it," he said. "I'm not certain exactly what the spells were, but it was quite discordant."

Cousins spat. "I should've guessed he would try something suitably clever." He paused for a moment, but Ian pulled him along. "This visit was a *complete* waste of time, then. You know, we should just go back there and…"

"Not today, my young warrior," Ian interrupted. "We achieved all we needed: we let Favo see us, and we saw the inside of his building. He now knows we are not to be trifled with, and I was able to reinforce a certain spell I've had to cast on him several times over the past few years. On another topic, however, you should know that we are being followed."

Cousins sighed. He wasn't yet convinced the trip hadn't been a total loss. But being trailed in the open on the streets? That might at least provide some much-needed entertainment. Or, potentially, information.

CPSIA information can be obtained at www.ICGtesting.com
Printed in the USA
LVOW06s1923240815

451321LV00001B/77/P